STAY ALIVE

CAVE-IN

STAY ALIVE

CAVE-IN

JOSEPH MONNINGER

SCHOLASTIC INC.

No part of this publication may be reproduced, stored in a retrieval system, or transmitted in any form or by any means, electronic, mechanical, photocopying, recording, or otherwise, without written permission of the publisher. For information regarding permission, write to Scholastic Inc., Attention: Permissions Department, 557 Broadway, New York, NY 10012.

ISBN 978-0-545-56352-9

12 11 10 9 8 7 6 5 4 3 2   14 15 16 17 18 19/0

Printed in the U.S.A.   40
First printing, April 2014

PART ONE
TREMORS

SURVIVAL TIP #1

If you are inside a building when an earthquake occurs, stay inside. Move to the center of the room or take a position underneath the frame of a doorway. Do not run outside. If you are outside, remain where you are. If you are driving a car, stop the car and stay inside the vehicle until the tremors cease. When the shaking stops, assess your status. Check to make sure electric fixtures have not loosened or become dangerous from the shaking. Remember that trees and walls, even entire buildings, might be damaged by tremors. Use extreme caution when moving about after an earthquake.

CHAPTER 1

Lobsterman Bertie Smith put the nose of the *Laurie Hall* on the rise of land at the center of Hog Island Ledge, Casco Bay, Maine, and set a course straight for her. Nothing to it. A bit of wind had come up from the east, turning the water milky, but it was an easy run to the island. He had done it before, plenty of times, in fact, but never with such a crew as the one he had on board today. When he looked back from the wheel, pretending to check behind him, he saw six kids stretched out, half of them already green around the gills with seasickness.

"Water is a little choppy," the teacher-boy said from his position beside the wheel.

"Guess so."

"We're supposed to have pretty good weather. That was the last report."

"It's November," Bertie said, stating the obvious. "Be cold out on that island."

"We're prepared for it," said the teacher with confidence.

"That so?"

The trip was a stupid idea, as anyone on Earth would know except the teacher-boy, Bertie reflected. You did not camp on Hog Island at the tail end of November if you had half an ounce of intelligence to begin with. It was just a long weekend, true, but pretty soon the bay would be thick as chowder and you could get a wind running over your back out there that you wouldn't soon forget. No, sir. The island sat exposed to every wind and curl of water. Seals used it more than people did. It held a working fort sometime around the Civil War, but that day had long since passed. That fort had been ancient when Bertie was a boy.

"Hey," the teacher-boy shouted back to the students, his voice hardly making it above the diesel chunk of the engine. "You all ready? You ready to camp? We're going to see some amazing birds. Puffins!"

The kids, some of them anyway, nodded. One made a little *whoo-hooooo* sound, but Bertie knew the kid was being a brat. Mostly they watched one of the boys fly a jury-rigged kite behind the boat. The boy had folded a piece of paper into a plane and put a string through its nose. Now it fluttered behind the boat, rising and falling on the air currents.

"Is that it?" the teacher-girl asked, coming into the cuddy and pointing toward the island. "Is that the island?"

Bertie nodded. The girl was a student teacher, he knew, working at the school beside the teacher-boy. He had talked to them both to arrange the transport. They made quite a pair, Bertie thought. At least the teacher-girl had the good sense to wear a wool hat for the crossing. The teacher-boy didn't even have that much sense.

"Do many boats come out this way?" the teacher-girl asked.

"In the summer, some do," Bertie said. "Not many this time of year. You've got the ferry line out to Peaks Island."

"How about tankers and such?" the teacher-boy asked.

"They'd be farther out to sea. And the fishing trade shuts down this time of year, 'cepting for the lobster boys, and they stick closer to shore. Oh, you'll have the island to yourselves, you can count on that."

The teacher-girl smiled at receiving that information. The teacher-boy looked out the front windshield and went up on his toes to see the island over the curve of the sea. The island looked like an eyebrow, Bertie reflected, always had, always would.

Sam Harding watched the paper airplane flutter behind the boat. It was pretty cool. It rode the air currents and floated up and down, jerking and soaring in rhythms you couldn't predict. His mom was big on kite making. She had even opened a small business for a while out of their basement, designing homemade kites and huge origami swans, and just about anything else that could be made from paper. She named the business Folds, which was not a good name for a business, because pretty soon it *did* fold, and people couldn't resist making jokes about it.

"Hey, Sam, why don't you tie this on the plane?" Harry Cameron asked.

Sam looked down at Harry. Harry had his fingers held in a circle below his knee. Sam had made the mistake of looking, and he watched Harry give a satisfied smile and begin climbing toward him over the luggage. By looking at the finger circle, Sam had given Harry the right to punch him in the shoulder. It was the oldest game going, and it had circulated around their school like a virus the last few weeks.

Sam closed his eyes and leaned forward to accept his punishment.

Harry punched him hard on the shoulder, but not ridiculously hard, as some people did. After the punch Sam felt a dull ache begin in his deltoid, the muscle that covered his shoulder.

"This is sick," Harry said, pushing down onto the deck of the boat beside Sam. "It's going to be cold as anything out there."

Harry's breath smelled like peanut butter, Sam realized. Harry's breath usually smelled like peanut butter.

"You seasick at all?" Sam asked, mostly because he felt a little seasick and wouldn't have minded hearing someone else say he felt funny.

"Naw, I'm okay."

"Sandy looks like she's going to yak," Sam said, pushing his chin a little at Sandy Bellow, the most annoying girl in the world.

"Sandy's not exactly outdoorsy."

"I don't even know why she's on this trip."

"Neither does she, I bet."

Sam pulled the line tighter on the paper airplane. It looked pretty cool the way it navigated the air currents. Harry stood up quickly and looked in the direction the boat was heading. Then he sat back down. Sam kept his eyes on the airplane.

"We're getting there," Harry said. "Shouldn't be long now."

"Five days on an island."

"It'll be cool."

"You think so? I guess," Sam said.

Sam let out the last of his string. The plane went higher, but it also swooped lower, threatening to dive into the backwash behind the boat. He looked around at the other kids. Bob Worm watched the plane, but Sandy sat with her hoodie up over her head, her hands stuffed in the front pouch pocket; Mary and Azzy played some sort of card game down low, but the cards blew around and scattered whenever the wind could pry them up. The two teachers, Mr. O'Connell and Ms. Carpenter, stood up by the captain of the boat. The wind sometimes brought their voices over the sound of the engine.

The boat quartered a little and the wind changed. Sam's plane dipped down and the string ran against Sandy's head. In one quick motion she reached up and knocked the string away and the plane snapped free. It sputtered for a moment, almost surprised, Sam thought, to find itself no longer attached to the string, then it rose up and backward for an instant before finally plunging into the sea.

"Way to go, Sandy," Harry said.

"Keep it out of my face," she said, not looking up.

Then the engine sound softened and Sam heard the gulls begin calling like crazy.

Eamon O'Connell, seventh-grade advisor and social-science teacher, went to the stern of the boat and tried to gauge the rock of the sea. It *was* choppy, that was for sure. Choppier than he had anticipated. When Bertie had said he would have to off-load on the lee side, wherever that happened to be, Eamon had simply taken it for granted that there would be a lee side. A calm side. But now, with the wind up and the sea churning, Eamon saw he had underestimated the very first element of the camping trip.

"Looks like we're going to get wet," Ursula, his student teacher, observed. "What's your plan?"

He wanted to say, *Plan? What plan?*

But he knew that wouldn't inspire confidence.

"You need to make a move," Bertie said, shouting over the engine noises. "I can't hold her here for long."

"It's not deep," Eamon said, reassuring himself as much as anything else.

"It's cold, though," Ursula said. "They'll be cold by the time we make it to land if they have to wade in."

"Not sure what else we can do. I thought we could land on the beach, but Bertie says no," Eamon said. "I'll go first."

It wasn't a good plan. Eamon saw that right away. But he was in charge, it was his program to run, so he slipped out of his backpack and got ready to climb over the edge. Once he was over the edge and secured his footing, then he could help the others. At the same time he worried that the boat, bobbing and chucking on the sea, could back up and smash him against the rocks. He wondered what he had been thinking, taking six students to a deserted island on Thanksgiving weekend.

He felt the students gathered at the stern to watch him. Sam and Harry stood side by side, and the girls, Azzy, Mary, and Sandy, huddled together against the wind. Bob Worm stood at the rear of the grouping, taller and wider than any of the others.

Eamon decided to put a bold face on a bad situation.

"Okay, I'm hopping in," he said. "It's only about knee deep. We can make a chain and hand the bags up. Ursula, if you don't mind, you can be the last one off. You can make sure everyone gets off okay."

"Get a move on!" Bertie shouted.

Eamon slid over the stern, dangled for a second on the gunwale, then pushed back and dropped onto his feet. The cold took his breath away. The water lapped against him and nearly knocked him off his pins, but then he braced himself for balance and smiled up at the students.

"Nothing to it," he said. "Who's next?"

Bob Worm knew what they would ask even before they asked it.

People *always* asked. Just because he was big, sort of gigantic, really, for his grade, people always expected more from him. No, he reflected, that wasn't true. They expected more from him physically, absolutely, but they thought of him, by and large, as a big, solid dullard.

People held a prejudice against big kids and didn't even know it.

Right now, for instance, he stood in the water, freezing his tail off, while kids handed out their bags to him. Then he turned and handed the bags to Mr. O'Connell, who in turn handed the bags to Azzy, who in turn handed them to a revolving parade of people on the rocky shoreline. No one else had to stand in the water, no student anyway, unless you counted Azzy, who only stood in water up to her ankles. The big jobs, the big lifts, always fell on his shoulders, and Bob Worm hated it.

"Make sure you get everything," Mr. O'Connell called up to the boat.

Then he turned to the shoreline and yelled at the class.

"People, people, make sure your bag has been off-loaded. Make sure you have your gear. Check carefully. We don't want to leave anything behind."

Bob Worm knew the kids wouldn't check. That's just the way it went.

"Almost there," Ms. Carpenter, the student teacher, said from the boat. "You okay, Bob?"

"Getting cold," Bob Worm said.

"Hold on just a little longer."

She looked around the deck of the boat. Then she handed out a small camera bag. Bob Worm passed it back toward shore.

"Check your bags!" Ms. Carpenter yelled at the kids on the shoreline. "Make sure you have everything!"

Bob Worm watched a couple kids glance at the pile of backpacks and junk piled on the shoreline. They didn't do anything close to a thorough search.

"Okay, thanks, Mr. Smith," Ms. Carpenter yelled to the lobster guy. "That's it."

"See you Tuesday," Bertie Smith said. "Right around noon. If the weather turns ugly, it may be earlier or later. Be ready."

"Okay."

Ms. Carpenter climbed over the tail of the boat. The stern, Bob Worm reminded himself. Bow, stern, port, starboard.

She plunked into the water up to her waist and let out a little yelp. Bob Worm held out his hand, and she grabbed it and clambered toward shore. He followed her.

The lobster boat pulled out of the cove bit by bit. Bob Worm tasted the diesel exhaust on his tongue as he climbed onto Hog Island.

You didn't think the wind could blow as hard as it did, Harry Cameron thought, but then it did anyway. And it didn't stop. He felt the wind shoving at him, curling over the island top and *shoving at him*, as if it had decided it didn't want them to camp there.

"Whoaaaaa," he said to no one in particular at one huge gust.

He watched Ms. Carpenter clump onto the island. Then Bob Worm. Mr. O'Connell had already climbed up the hill toward the center of the island to scout. That's what he said. He was heading off scouting. That left everyone else standing in a circle around their bags, all of them facing away from the wind.

"Whoooaaaaaaaaa," Harry said again as the wind hit his back.

"I'm freeezinnnnnggggggggggg," Sandy Bellow said, her hat tucked down over her head and her hoodie up over her hat.

"We'll get out of the wind in a minute," Ms. Carpenter said in a teacher voice. "Just hold on. Let's all work together."

Harry flipped the hood of his hoodie up over his head.

He was freezing, too.

His pant legs were wet, for one thing. For another thing, the wind came across the island like a snarling wildebeest. If you cocked your head one way or the other, all you could hear was a high, desperate keening sound.

And birds.

Millions and millions of birds.

Well, okay, maybe not *millions* of birds, but certainly thousands. Mostly gulls. They glided back and forth above them, banking on the wind, calling, shouting, making all sorts of weird, haunted noises that sounded, in certain registers, like babies crying. It gave the whole scene a strange, haunted feeling.

He put his hand in his pocket and felt the harmonica resting there. He wanted to play it, but he thought it might look pretty corny to pull it out and start playing it right away. Still, he wondered what the gulls would think of harmonica music coming at them over the wind. He thought it might sound pretty cool.

He didn't have long to think, though, because Mr. O'Connell came charging down the hillside at that moment and yelled for everyone to come closer. Harry walked over toward the pile of bags, but found the bottoms of his pants had frozen into two tubes of ice. He punched his hand on his pant legs and shattered the ice.

"The old fort is right up there," Mr. O'Connell said, pointing up the hill. "We can find a place to be out of the wind. We can set up next to the fort wall. If we all work together, we can have a camp set up in an hour maybe."

"I'm freeezzzzzzing," Sandy said.

"I know, I know, sorry," Mr. O'Connell said. "It wasn't the ideal way to get off the boat, but we had to do what we did. Hope you all understand. Remember, no exploring the fort until everything is set up. Is that clear?"

Yes, that is clear, Harry thought.

"Okay, grab your own bag and as much of the other stuff as you can. We're almost there. Everyone pitch in. Aren't these birds amazing?"

Harry looked around the circle of students. What they thought was amazing, he knew, was that they were standing on an island off the coast of Maine on the day after Thanksgiving with the wind howling like an Irish demon and the birds calling for their blood.

CHAPTER 2

A zzy, Mary, Sam, Harry, Sandy, Bob. Check. Ursula
Carpenter, student teacher, mentally checked off
the student roll, then dumped her backpack beside the
wall of Fort Gorges and lifted her fleece away from her
belly. She had not wanted to sweat given the force of the
wind and the chill from the water, but the climb up
the hill had been a pain. The kids had whined and whee-
dled and tried to get out of carrying anything, and she
had taken up the slack by making three trips.

Gung-Ho Gussie. That's what her dad called her.
That's how he teased her.

She was always a little too ready to jump into the
fray. As a result, she had grabbed more than her share,
way more than her share, and had lugged things up the

incline to the foot of the fort. Now she dumped her back-pack and other junk and looked around.

It was good to be out of the wind. The wind could make you a little crazy, she thought, a little testy. Eamon didn't seem to mind, though. He jumped around and kept everyone's spirits up, laughing and joking and trying to get people to see the fun of the situation. The kids looked leery and doubtful, as if they couldn't quite believe what they had gotten involved in. They hadn't really approached their usual level of goofiness since the boat had left the dock on the mainland. They all looked a little stunned by their surroundings.

"Tents up," Eamon called. "Get your tents up and your sleeping bags inside. Remember to weight the tents and peg them down. The wind is going to try to take them out to sea."

"How do you do the tent?" Sandy asked.

Sandy always asked and played the "helpless" card. About everything.

"We went over this, Sandy," Eamon said, trying hard not to be exasperated. "Remember? In the gym?"

"Yeah, but . . ." Sandy said and looked around.

Do not help her, Ursula commanded herself. *Do not go over and help her.*

Ursula decided, instead, to get her own tent set up. They all had single-person tents, little snail shells, that Eamon had lobbied for with the school administration. Back in the day, she knew, they'd had large communal tents for the Outing Club, but Eamon had argued, correctly, she thought, that they were better off in small tents. No back-and-forthing, no sneaking into one another's tents, no goofing off in the middle of the night. It was a little less fun, perhaps, but much more organized and more secure. Besides, they could stay out beside the fire as long as they wanted, or at least fairly late, but when they turned in that was the end of the day.

She slipped her tent out of its stuff sack and rolled it out on the ground. It popped up with internal brackets. The only reason Sandy wouldn't be able to do it, Ursula realized, was because Sandy wouldn't try.

"How's it going?" Eamon asked, suddenly appearing beside her.

"It's okay. Just getting my tent up."

"I thought we were in big trouble with the landing," Eamon confessed in a lower voice. "Captain Bertie got a kick out of dumping us like that."

"You think so?"

Eamon nodded. Then he leaned closer.

"It's cold, isn't it?" he said. "I didn't want to say that to the kids. They're looking a little shell-shocked."

"I think we're all just chilled."

"I didn't want to tell them, but we can set up in the powder magazine if it gets really windy. The magazine is underground and it's lined with stones. It's probably pretty dirty, but it'd get us out of the wind."

"Powder magazine?" Ursula asked.

"Where they used to store munitions. In World War Two they kept submarine mines in it."

"Are we supposed to go in there?"

"You can wander around all you like. The city of Portland owns this land, but it's pretty much abandoned. We'll take a look once we get settled in."

"Okay."

"Thanks for helping with all the baggage. We need to have a little talk about group participation, don't we?"

"I guess so."

He left as she finished getting the form of the tent set up. The wind came up and nearly jerked it from her hands. She rolled her backpack into the toe of the tent. Then she unrolled her sleeping pad and fit it into the interior. It all worked, all fit together properly. She took a few minutes to sink pegs into the bony ground, then weighted the tent a little extra with rocks. When she finished, she looked up to see Sandy standing beside her, her face red and pinched.

"Can you help me?" Sandy asked.

Ursula, against her better judgment, nodded and followed Sandy back to her tent. Right next to her location, Mary had already erected her tent. Mary was the opposite of Sandy: independent, calm, competent. Ursula didn't like to admit it to herself, but Mary was a bit of a favorite. Ursula tried not to show any favoritism, but when confronted by Sandy on one side and Mary on the other, it was nearly impossible not to fall into it.

"How are you doing, Mary?" Ursula asked before she helped Sandy.

"It's beautiful here," Mary said from her knees. She had been jamming her backpack into her tent, but she stopped to look around. "I love the ocean."

"It *is* beautiful," Ursula agreed and admired her view of the sea. "We're going to have a great time here."

"I'm already having a great time," Mary said.

Ursula grew aware of Sandy beside her, impatient and needy.

"It's cold, is what it is," Sandy said.

"We each make our own world," Ursula said, which was a phrase her dad used on her whenever she became cranky. "Try to be cheerful, Sandy. Things will work better that way."

"I'm cooollddddddd," Sandy whined.

Ursula took a deep breath to calm herself. Then she told Sandy to grab the other end of the tent and to roll it out carefully.

Sam Harding played the movie game with himself as he set up his tent. It went like this:

Scene: Maine island.

Cast: Kids doing a community service project. Superenthusiastic teacher/bird lover.

Conflict: Cold, wind, severe weather conditions.

Plot?

He couldn't think of a plot. Not yet. As he popped open the tent, then pegged it down, he considered that this was a situational movie, not a character movie. A situational movie was the type where the situation was the most important element. Like *Gravity*, maybe, or like *Jurassic Park*. You put characters in a difficult environment, applied pressure, and voilà. You had a movie. Zombie movies generally relied on the situation, not character, to carry them forward.

You could make a wizard zombie movie on the island, he thought. Great light, great bird sounds. And the wind could almost become a character all itself.

Meanwhile, he had to blow on his hands to keep them warm. He had forgotten gloves. He had them next to his backpack when he was packing, but somehow between there and here he had lost them. Maybe in his mom's car. Maybe in the white Cedarbrook van. One way or the other, he had lost them, and now his fingers felt thick as breakfast sausages as he tried to work on the tent.

"How's everyone doing?" Mr. O'Connell asked, coming around. "Tents up? Anyone having a problem?"

"Nope," Sam said under his breath. "No problem."

He finished getting his tent up, then slid his sleeping pad and sleeping bag inside. *A little cocoon*, he thought. Then he put his backpack inside and lashed up the door. Done. He stood and looked around.

It wasn't really that bad. The place, he meant.

Actually, it was kind of cool. He knew the kids complained a lot and made a big deal about having to camp on the island for a community service project, but it also was a little adventure. They had to clean up the island so the nest sites would be ready when the puffins returned in the spring. Everything was about puffins; Mr. O'Connell was nuts about them, and he was some sort of grand puffin king at the Audubon Society. Everyone at Cedarbrook gave Mr. O'Connell toy puffins, or emailed him video links because that's what you did to butter up a teacher. Even the headmaster made jokes about puffins, and it was all har-de-har-har whenever the school had an assembly, because you could count on some sort of puffin joke becoming a running theme. Sam didn't have anything against puffins, but he didn't have anything *for* them, either, at least not in any special way. He was along for the ride, that was all, and for the credits he could get for community service on his permanent record.

"How you doing, Sam?" Ms. Carpenter asked from where she was helping Sandy Bellow set up her tent. "You all squared away?"

"I think so."

"Make sure you have plenty of weight to hold it down. This wind is something, isn't it?"

"Yes."

"Reminds me of Hitchcock's *The Birds*. You ever see it, Sam?"

Sam shook his head.

"Great film," Ms. Carpenter said and then turned her attention back to Sandy Bellow.

"I bet," Sam said, but he was pretty sure the wind carried his voice away and dumped it in the ocean.

"Come on over, come on over, up here!" Mr. O'Connell called.

Azzy jogged over to where the group had collected by the wall of the fort. Azzy always jogged, ever since she had read an article about a national champion wrestler from Iowa. The guy was old school, sure, but he jogged everywhere, never walked, and he claimed it was the reason he had become a champion. When all else failed, you could always outwork the next person, and Azzy – a three-sport athlete: ice hockey, lacrosse, and soccer – knew that recipe to be true. She was always in better shape than anyone she played against. That much was a given.

So she jogged up the hill to where everyone crowded around Mr. O'Connell. He had found a small rock to stand on and he had a happy, somewhat goofy look on his face. The Puffin Master. That's what kids called him. Azzy stopped on the outside of the small circle. The wind slammed down at them, but closer in, beside the building's wall, the wind didn't possess as much strength. Everyone seemed to understand that and they crowded forward, trying to get out of the cutting air, until Mr. O'Connell held up his hand.

"That means 'quiet,'" he said. "That means I'm requesting quiet. It's an old Cub Scout thing."

"Everyone quiet," Ms. Carpenter said. "Hand is up."

Azzy thought, *Cub Scouts? Really?*

Coach Clemins would have laughed at that, she reflected. Coach Clemins would have howled.

"We made it!" Mr. O'Connell said. "I know the landing wasn't perfect, but we're here. It was okay, right? We're here for five days and four nights. Bertie is going to pick us up Tuesday afternoon. Anyone have any questions on the schedule?"

No one had any questions on the schedule, Azzy knew.

"Okay, then," Mr. O'Connell went on. "Well, welcome to Hog Island Ledge. As you can see, it's pretty remote. We are on our own, yeah!"

He waited for a rallying response, but none came.

"Our job over the next few days is to prepare nesting sites. The currents are wicked strong around this island, so they pull in all kinds of stuff. Lobster traps, driftwood, plastic bottles, you name it. When the puffins come back in the spring, they won't establish nests if we don't clean up a little. So it's pretty simple, really. We're going to start at the far end of the ledge and clean this way, bringing everything down. What we can burn off, we will. We can have some great bonfires. But the plastics and other materials, well, we'll collect those and load them up when Captain Bertie comes back for us. Any questions?"

"When do we start?" Sandy Bellow asked.

"Now, really. We're going to divide into two teams. Boys with me, girls with Ms. Carpenter. First, though, I'm going to take you on a little tour. This fort behind me is called Fort Gorges. It was planned after the War of 1812 and then built finally around the Civil War. It's on the National Registry, but it's not a creaky antique. We're free to roam around it as much as we like."

Azzy listened with half her attention. The rest of her attention drifted away to the fort. It was a huge stone mass, shaped, she knew, in a *D*. The rounded part of the *D* pointed out toward the ocean. The rear flat shape stared back at the mainland. Her dad, Edgar, said the fort was haunted. He said everyone knew the fort was haunted, and he was surprised the teacher – he didn't know Mr. O'Connell's name offhand – would bring a bunch of kids out there on Thanksgiving weekend. It was haunted by plenty of ghosts, her dad said, but most particularly by Whistling Willy, a peg-legged ghost with a cannonball in his guts and a single eye that dangled from the socket when he bent over.

That eye, her dad said, *hangs from a Slinky. Just like it. That eye comes out and slithers toward you.*

It was ridiculous. And also kind of creepy.

"Okay, are we good?" Mr. O'Connell asked. "We ready to take a look around?"

"Someone said there is a powder magazine out here," Harry Cameron yelled. "Is that true?"

Harry, Azzy knew, was a nut about explosives. A powder magazine was a little piece of heaven to him.

"You'll see, you'll see," Mr. O'Connell yelled, jumping down off the rock. "Five minutes. Assemble here."

Azzy nodded. She turned and jogged back to her tent. As she went she couldn't deny that she heard a thin, high sound among the birds calling. It sounded like a whistle, like Whistling Willy saying hello.

CHAPTER 3

Sandy Bellow hated everything about the island. And about the powder magazine, whatever it was. And about the gulls. And about the sleeping bags. And tents. And toilets . . .

Check that. There *were* no toilets.

Five days with no toilets. No showers. No heat.

How was this possible? That was what she thought as she followed Ms. Carpenter around the edge of the fort toward the back side of the island. She had been miserable before in her life, plenty of times, but this set a new record. This was one for the ages. She wondered why anyone on Earth would prefer to be here rather than in a tidy, candle-scented mall on this of all days.

Black Friday. The biggest shopping day of the year. She hated her life.

Actually, that wasn't true. She hated her *stepdad*. She hated Lenny, with his long sideburns, his weird, 1950s flattop hair, his honey-I'm-home flannel shirts. She hated him with a fury that made her ears burn.

"That wind really bites, doesn't it?" Ms. Carpenter asked everyone in their little marching brigade. "It cuts right through you."

"It does," someone said.

Sandy nodded. She couldn't risk saying anything for fear of wind zooming down her throat and freezing her tonsils. Lenny would have laughed. Lenny the evil stepdad, who said things like *Be darn good for her to get a little fresh air in her lungs.*

Be a step in the right direction to put some Spackle on her tail.

Spackle on her tail? What did that even mean? Sandy wondered.

So here she was. After relatively little conversation, and certainly no significant opposition from her mom – *Honey, you never know, it might be good for you and you get credits and it looks great on your record and it's not too early to start thinking about that* – trekking behind Ms. Carpenter and the other idiots who planned to spend the long, long, long weekend on this forsaken island.

"Oh, look at that!" Mr. O'Connell exclaimed from the front of the pack. "Just look at that. Look at that sun!"

Sandy followed the eyeline of the group and saw the sun ticking down over the trees to the west. It established a pretty trail along the water, she acknowledged, but it did not do a single thing for the wind that buffeted them like a puff of polar-bear breath. Actually, no, she decided, polar-bear breath would be warm. This was far, far colder than that.

"Does it seem cold to you?" Sandy asked Mary Eihorn, who happened to stand beside her.

"What?" Mary asked, her eyes fixed on the slanting light scraping across the ocean waves.

"Cold to you?" Sandy repeated.

Mary shrugged. Mary the back-to-earth moon child. Mary, the kid who got dropped off at school by a pair of parents driving a VW Westfalia, a camping thingy from the 1970s. *That* Mary.

"Not that cold," Mary said, slowly drawing her eyes back from the beginning of the sunset. "I've been in worse."

"But that doesn't mean it isn't cold, right? I mean, just because you've been in worse doesn't mean it isn't cold right here, right now, right?"

Mary smiled. And didn't answer.

Sandy suspected she had been whining. She whined a lot, she knew. At least that's what other people said. Frankly, she considered it a case of submitting her opinion to the world, but that was only her own opinion.

Lenny always said she whined.

After sufficient *ooooooh*s *and aaaaaah*s, Sandy followed the group toward the fort. A gull banked in the wind directly over her head and pooped down on the crowd. The stream landed on Mary's shoulder, which gave Sandy a certain amount of happiness. But Mary simply reached to the side of the trail, grabbed a clump of grass, wadded it to make a small sponge, and wiped her shoulder clean. She didn't seem to care. When she finished, she tossed the grass away and didn't even inspect her coat.

Sandy worked her way into the center of the group. At least there, she figured, the wind wouldn't be as bad and the gulls would have more trouble finding her.

Mary Eihorn ducked her head down and stepped into the powder magazine and looked around. It was sort of amazing. She wasn't entirely sure what she had expected it to look like, but it wasn't like this. It was a long stone building, built into the earth. You could not see it from above. The roof had grown over with weedy grass a long time ago, and unless you looked for it you would have missed it altogether. Someone had said when they first stepped inside that it looked like a baseball dugout, the major-league type, and that was probably as good a description as any. Except it was constructed with stone. And it was far away from the fort on purpose.

In case it blew up.

That's what Mr. O'Connell said. He also pointed at the floor, rotted and eaten up now, but once upon a time made of wood. The wood had no nails, Mr. O'Connell said. Nothing that could cause a spark. Sparks could ignite gunpowder. And gunpowder was what you kept in a powder magazine.

"Doesn't it feel good to be out of the wind?" Mr. O'Connell asked at the front of the group. "Go ahead, you all can look around. Just mind your step. Be careful. This is an old, old building, and it's badly weathered. Don't stand on the roof. You might come right through it."

Mary reached in her pocket and pulled out a headlamp. It was dim inside the magazine. She put the headlamp on and walked slowly around the perimeter, close to the walls. People had tagged it with initials and names inside of hearts. And swearwords, names of teams, graduating classes, who had visited, what they thought of things . . . the usual stuff. Mary didn't understand the impulse to deface a building. What struck her most was the fact that you had to plan it out: first think about it long enough to care, then buy a can of paint, or ten cans of paint, get yourself to the location, then sneak around and spray your name on a wall that no one saw or cared about anyway. What was the point? It seemed boring to her.

At the east side of the powder magazine, she smelled something gross. Better to avoid that corner. She veered away and went back to the west. A few slots at eye level allowed people inside to look out, probably to check for ships, but for the most part the place was solidly underground. It felt like somebody's old, old basement, except no house rested on top of it.

She was still inspecting the walls with her headlamp when the first tremor hit.

It was strange. That was her first reaction. Very strange. You counted on the world to be solid and dependable, but then, suddenly, the world shook just enough to remind you that you lived on a blue marble flying through space, and that blue marble had various flaws and imperfections, and it was silly to imagine it would always be stable.

Except that's what you thought. That's what everyone thought. Until you didn't.

The floor began to heave and move and the walls, even these huge stone walls, she realized, had started to shake. It went on and on. Probably it was only a few seconds, but it felt like a million billion years, everything shaking and dancing, and for the tiniest instant she nearly convinced herself the wind had caused everything. Strong winds, very strong winds. But the shake came up from the ground, you felt it in your feet and in your guts, and the magazine was made of stone. Rock. Dirt. Wind couldn't do much to it.

Then everything became quiet. Supernaturally quiet. That was the strangest thing of all, she thought. She looked around, her headlamp catching the expressions of people near her. Some looked scared; others looked bewildered. Mr. O'Connell held his hands in front of him like a person walking down a dark hallway. And Bob Worm, the giant Bob Worm, had turned crazily into a karate stance, ready to combat whatever came at him. It made her smile to see him, because only Bob Worm would figure you could karate chop a tremor, and she kept her headlamp beam on him for a three count.

And then someone screamed.

Azzy ran at the first tremble. She didn't think about it, didn't evaluate her options, but ran instead. As simple as that. As animal as that. Her whole impulse, her whole desire, was *OUT.*

GET ME OUT.

The powder magazine made her claustrophobic to begin with, reaaaallyyyyy claustrophobic, and she couldn't stand thinking about all the *weight* around her. All the stone and dirt. It was like being inside a grave, an enormous grave, and she hated everything about it. She didn't care how cold it was outside, or how hard the wind blew; she wanted to be anywhere but inside the powder magazine.

Added to that, of course, the entire structure danced. It moved. *What was that?* she wondered as her legs began to pump and move her toward the door. She didn't examine the angles or decide consciously on a best plan. She ran. Like a deer at a rifle shot. Like a horse at a snake. If it were possible, she would have kicked up her feet like hooves and tried to kick the stuffing out of the magazine. Because she didn't like the magazine. Not a bit.

And she sure as heck didn't like the shake.

Then it all became a little like a slo-mo sequence in a cheesy movie. She saw people near her turn, or look up, or hold out their hands to balance themselves, and she nearly knocked over Harry Cameron, the kid who kept playing the circle-finger-punch-in-the-shoulder game, on her dash to the door. But the door canted sideways a little, *moved*, and doors, particularly stone doors, did not do that in her experience. She kept running. And her legs felt funny because the ground underneath her moved. It moved. It swayed, she thought, like a magic carpet might sway if you tried to stand on it and run, but she kept going, feeling a little dizzy as she went, and then the bright rectangle of the door began to close.

How? How did the door close? That was impossible. The door didn't have a door, which sounded peculiar, even to her – a door without a door? – but it was simply an opening into the magazine. It was not a true doorway with a closable door. She ran at it anyway, ignoring the critical part of her mind that thought she might be making a mistake. Someone behind her screamed, a girl, a shrieky girl's voice, and that only made her run faster.

When she hit the doorway, she felt like a fish rising,

like a fish going up in the water column, hooray, food, safety, escape, and she glanced up at the late-afternoon light and missed entirely the block of granite that had chosen that precise instant to fall free from the overhead structure. It had been resting in the same spot for about a century and a half, waiting, on the top of the powder magazine. Grass had grown on the uphill side, but water had trenched around it, creating a tiny ramp beneath it, so that when the tremor hit the building it was just enough to get it moving. It tipped forward and rolled, but even then it would have stopped if it hadn't been near winter. The soil on the downhill side had turned icy in the late-fall weather, and the rock, once moving, slid forward with increasing speed.

It leaped off the roof and skidded out for a half foot until gravity took it and smacked it earthward. Then it fell.

It weighed seventy-four pounds, and it hit Azzy with such force that she did not feel it. Then more rocks fell – not that she noticed; she was finished noticing things – and the doorway began to close, stone by stone, like tremendously large bits of sand falling through an hourglass and filling up the bottom globe.

PART TWO
A TONGUE OF STONE

SURVIVAL TIP #2

During a cave-in, or if you become lost in a cave, conserve your light. Turn off flashlights when you are not moving, and use only one at a time. Form a chain of people following the one with a flashlight. If you're using a headlamp, use the lowest-output setting. Remember: darkness in underground caverns can be absolute. When most people think of "the dark," they usually imagine they can see something. That is not the case underground. Nothing will be a greater blow to group morale than darkness. Light is essential and is as valuable as water or food in these instances.

CHAPTER 4

Bob Worm listened to the last stones fall. It was intense. Everything had gone from zero to one hundred in seconds. Someone had screamed – was *still* screaming, as a matter of fact – and someone had just disappeared under rocks. Azzy, he thought, though he couldn't be sure. He couldn't be sure of much, truthfully, except that the entire powder magazine had nearly collapsed.

Dust everywhere. And far away, like water turning off in an apartment above you, the stones continued to trickle down. More dust. It looked like a cheesy haunted house with all the dust swirling around.

"Hey," someone called. "Hey!"

But the person didn't say anything afterward. They just said *Hey*.

Bob Worm didn't trust himself to move. He didn't want to move. Movement meant jeopardy, and he didn't want to take so much as a step. Things could still fall, he knew. Things could all fall down, just like the nursery rhyme went – *ashes, ashes, we all fall down* – and blundering forward would only put him in more peril.

Besides, he wasn't entirely sure where forward might be.

Locating forward meant understanding where backward was, and he couldn't be sure of that, either.

"Hey," the person kept yelling. "Hey."

A snow globe, Bob Worm thought. That's what it reminded him of now. A snow globe, only it wasn't gentle white snow that fell, but dirt and pebbles and stones. Lots of stone.

Slowly, slowly, moving his head only, he looked to his right. That was where the scream came from. He saw Sandy Bellow on her knees, her hands up to cover her face, her mouth a siren. She screamed like an air-raid whistle from one of the old WWII documentaries he liked to watch. Her voice went on and on and on.

"Quiet," he whispered.

She kept going.

"Quiet, Sandy. You're not helping," he said.

She looked at him. Her eyes had bugged out – he had always thought that was just a phrase, but he knew better now – and her mouth kept moving around the scream as if her lips wrapped around the sound as it passed.

Sam Harding got to his knees slowly. A stone had knocked him off his feet. A big stone. It had rammed into his right shoulder, nearly breaking it, and it had skinned flesh from his ear. He couldn't really think straight, couldn't assess what had happened. First there had been a shake, then everything had let loose. He had never been in an earthquake before; he wasn't sure he had been in one now. If this magazine still had some gunpowder left in it, it could have been an explosion for all he knew.

"What was that?" he asked, not really expecting an answer.

"It was an earthquake," someone said.

"Are you sure?"

"How do I know?" the person replied.

It was Bob Worm talking.

Sam nodded. The rock had taken his glasses from his head, he realized.

"IS EVERYONE OKAY? IS EVERYONE HERE?"

That was Mr. O'Connell. That was him shouting.

"Azzy . . ." Bob Worm said, but didn't finish his thought.

Everything appeared cloudy, Sam thought. He couldn't get a good look at anything. Dust swirled in the dimness and little specks of stone and dirt continued to fall. He felt something hot and bright on his bicep, his right bicep, and when he looked down he discovered the stone had ripped his sleeve away. Blood dripped from his arm. His skin looked like it had been run back and forth on a cheese grater. He wiggled his fingers to make sure they still worked. They did, but slowly.

"Azzy . . ." Bob Worm said again.

What about *Azzy?* Sam thought. He couldn't focus. The dust was disorienting. It was almost possible to imagine up was down, and down was up.

Then Ms. Carpenter appeared out of the dust, her face stretched tight with worry, her eyes blinking.

"Sam, you okay?" she asked quietly.

He nodded.

He wasn't okay, but he nodded anyway. He wasn't sure why, but he suspected it had something to do with Azzy. He was okay compared to Azzy. He wasn't sure how he knew that, but he did.

"Bob, you okay?" she asked Bob Worm.

Bob nodded. He didn't say anything.

"That was an earthquake," Mr. O'Connell called. "It had to be. That was an earthquake!"

Ms. Carpenter bent close and looked at Sam's arm.

"That must hurt," she said.

Ironically, it hadn't hurt until she said it must. Then it hurt like the devil. He felt it pulsing in time to his heart.

"It hurts a little," Sam said.

"We'll look at it in a second. First we have to check

on everyone, okay? Just hold on a second. I know you're in pain."

She left. The dust took her. Yes, it was dreamlike, Sam admitted. The effect would be almost too cheesy to use in a movie, but it worked here. Imagine Dracula going back into his grave, or down the stairs into the dungeon. It worked like that.

Whoever had been yelling *Hey!* finally stopped.

That was a relief, Sam thought. He needed to look down at his arm again, but he didn't really want to do it. He didn't want to *see* it. He worried he was mangled, and mangled *bad*. He had once brought a robin into the house after a UPS truck had hit it. The robin had jumped around, obviously in shock and alarm, but it kept fluttering futilely in circles. The broken wing dangled from the root of the intact wing like a balloon tied around a kid's wrist. It was horrible to look at.

He didn't want to see *that*.

"Everyone is accounted for except Azzy," Ursula whispered to Eamon O'Connell. They stood slightly removed from the group of students they had gathered in front of them. For reasons she did not entirely understand, Ursula found it easy to be calm. At least to *sound* calm. Inside, her stomach felt anything but calm.

"Is she . . . ?" Eamon started to ask, but didn't finish the sentence.

"No way to know. She ran outside."

"Did she make it?"

Ursula shrugged. She had been shrugging a lot in the past three or so minutes.

"Of all the places to be during a quake," Eamon said, "this might be one of the worst."

"If we stay calm, we'll be all right."

"Maybe," Eamon said. "Yes, yes, sure. Sorry. Yes, we'll stay calm."

"We should talk to them."

"We will."

"*You* should," Ursula said. "This is your project."

"You know we might be trapped in here?" he whispered.

"We might be, but we don't know yet. We'll have to see. Sam's arm is bleeding pretty badly. He's a risk for shock."

"Is anyone else hurt?"

"Nothing too serious. Bumps and bruises."

Ursula watched Eamon nod. She wondered if this was the moment when she should reach over and slap him. *Wake up*, she wanted to scream into his face. But she doubted that would instill confidence in the kids. He seemed foggy and unsure of what came next.

Then the ground began to shake again.

Someone – Sandy – let out a giant scream. It went up and down Ursula's spine and rang some sort of internal bell. It made everything horrible. If she could have thrown a tomahawk of silence in that instant, she would have done it. But she couldn't and Sandy's voice went up and up and up until it could have been a genuine siren cranked to report the tremor.

The room shook. A gazillion pounds of rocks and dirt on a small island in Maine rocked up and down like the back of a shying horse. Ursula didn't move except to bring her hands out in front of her. Her eyes passed over the students and their eyes passed back at her and everyone exchanged a look as if to ask, *Is this really happening?*

But it *was* happening. The rocks began sliding again, shifting, and Ursula heard the grating sound and thought of molars. Big teeth. Teeth grinding at night – a gnarly, horrible sound. Dirt fell through the roof and landed in pitter-pats of soft sighs. The floor continued to buck and sway until finally the room quieted and the only sound left in the world was Sandy Bellow screaming her fool head off.

"Stop, Sandy," Ursula said.

Sandy didn't stop. Sandy kept screaming, higher and higher, until finally Mary Eihorn took a step toward her and slapped her straight across the face. Then the sound stopped. It stopped and left nothing in its place.

"We can't get out," Ursula heard Eamon say behind her. "We're trapped."

CHAPTER 5

The next tremor came as Mary Eihorn was handing a stone to Harry Cameron. Harry was supposed to hand it to Sandy Bellow, who handed it to Bob Worm, who lobbed it about a dozen feet to the left of the doorway. A daisy chain. A chain gang. Mary couldn't remember the proper name for it, but her family had *always* made a chain when they had to bring cordwood in for the winter. It was the best way to move a lot of little things with a minimum of effort. It could almost be fun, she knew, but that was on a bright fall day when you had an apple pie baking in the house, the good smells drifting out to you and making you happy to be busy. *Apple days*, her dad called those kinds of perfect

New England days. They had spent a lot of apple days passing wood hand-to-hand into the basement.

But the powder magazine was a different story.

She stopped for a moment when the tremor came. It was less definite than the earlier two. It passed quickly, like summer thunder going away over the mountains. The ground shook and chattered. No, it wasn't like summer thunder, Mary thought. It was like a giant walking slowly away, each footfall becoming softer with distance.

"That was another tremor," Harry Cameron said, his hand out to receive the stone Mary had ready to give him. "An aftershock."

Everyone had stopped, she saw. Even Mr. O'Connell and Ms. Carpenter had stopped tending Sam. They had Sam stretched out on the floor, a couple jackets underneath him. They had borrowed her headlamp so they could see his wounds. Only one light among them, Mary knew. The rest of the stuff – headlamps, water, food, even a satellite phone – waited for them out by the tents. No one had thought there was any need to bring a headlamp on a quick excursion to see the powder magazine.

Now they knew better.

"Stay calm," Mr. O'Connell said. "That's just an aftershock."

"I hate it," Sandy Bellow said.

"We should be okay now," Mr. O'Connell said. "That should be the last of it. If anything else comes, it will be softer."

"What about tsunamis?" Harry asked.

Mr. O'Connell didn't answer for a second. They all listened to the last tiny tremor move off still farther. A few small rocks, pebbles, really, fell onto the ground from the roof above.

"I doubt tsunamis are an issue here," Mr. O'Connell said carefully.

"Why not?" Sandy asked. "We're on an island, aren't we?"

She said "aren't we" with enough venom and scorn to make Mary's hair stand up on the back of her neck. She tried to feel sorry for slapping Sandy earlier, but she simply couldn't. That girl deserved to be slapped about every ten minutes.

"We're not at the edge of a geological plate," Ms. Carpenter said. "We're in the center of a plate. To get the really big waves, you need a huge upheaval down deep. I don't think what we experienced is on that scale."

Just enough to lock us into a vault underground, Mary thought. *Just that.*

"Let's keep moving stones," Mary said, handing Harry the stone she had been holding since the tremor started. "Let's control what we can control."

It was almost entirely dark. The last rays of twilight came in through the slots that looked out to the sea. The light lent everything a hazy, imperfect outline. One of the slots had shut, collapsed from above with the weight of the shift. Only one slot remained, but it appeared sturdy and solid and at least, Mary thought, they wouldn't have to worry about suffocation. That was off the table. But everything else was on the table: no food, no water, no consistent light, no latrines, no anything.

Those items were very much on the table.

She worked another five minutes, trying to be smart about which rocks she removed. The trick, she knew, was to have a plan for the removal. If you simply grabbed any old rock and passed it backward, then you might inadvertently work against yourself. Rocks could slide and fill in empty spaces. This job was like Jenga, the game in which you kept carefully lifting off pieces of wood and placing them on top, creating a tippy, unstable tower. Her headlamp would have helped a good deal to determine which rocks to select, but she had to be satisfied to squint in the near darkness and do her best. They needed to use the headlamp on Sam. Sam was pretty messed up.

She did not even want to think about Azzy.

"Hey, could everybody come over?" Mr. O'Connell asked, his voice soft and consoling. "Could you hold on and let's take a second?"

Mary stopped picking at the stones. She heard Bob Worm toss the last of the rocks into the pile to the left of the door. It was terribly dark now. She walked carefully toward Mr. O'Connell's voice. He wore the headlamp, she saw. It flashed wherever he looked.

"Okay," he said quietly, "everyone here? Look around you. . . . Check on the person next to you. Everyone okay?"

Because he had asked no individual, no one answered.

"We're okay, I think," Mary said for the group. "Just shaken up."

"No pun intended," Bob Worm interjected.

Mr. O'Connell apparently realized the headlamp had been painful to their eyes, so he slipped it off and put it in the center, beam facing up. *The world's smallest campfire*, Mary thought. Still, it was comforting to have some light.

"I won't kid you at all," Mr. O'Connell said when they had all settled. "You know we're in a bit of a pickle. No one could have predicted an earthquake. They just don't have much impact up here in Maine as a rule. As a rule."

He faded off, seemingly thinking of something. Then he cleared his throat and went on.

"This is what we know. We've had an earthquake. The tremors have gotten increasingly lighter, so I don't think we're in danger of more significant shocks. But as you know, some of the damage a quake does depends on where you are when it arrives. We happened to be in a powder magazine, and an old one at that. Not a great place to be, it turns out."

Mary heard Sandy snort. Apparently Sandy needed to underline any statements about their predicament with disgust.

"The good news is, other than Sam here, we all made it through unharmed. I know some of you are concerned about Azzy, and so am I. But we can't do anything about her for the moment. I'm sorry. It's possible she made it out and is trying to get help."

Mary cocked her head at that one. That was a fib Mr. O'Connell was telling them to make them feel better. She didn't appreciate being lied to, even for a good cause. If Azzy had made it out, it was likely they would have heard her calling. Or she would have gone around to the slot, where she could look inside. Something. Mary didn't buy Mr. O'Connell's explanation, but she didn't say anything.

"So, we need to get out of this magazine. I think Mary's idea to move the rocks is a good one. Let's keep doing that. It's hard to judge how thick the pile of fallen rocks might be. Mary, can you give us any insight?"

"Not yet, really," Mary said. "It's hard to see and it's a huge pile."

"But it's loose stone at least," Ms. Carpenter said. "We have that going for us."

"Hooray," Bob Worm said mockingly, but no one laughed.

"I wish we had some dynamite," Harry Cameron said. "I really do."

"Fantasies aside," Mr. O'Connell said patiently, his voice surfing the last of Harry's ridiculous notion, "our job has become digging out of here. Plain and simple. On Tuesday, Bertie will be back for us. We should be out long before that, but that's something we have on our side, too. And parents will begin to ask questions if we're not back . . . so it's not as if we can't expect the cavalry to come over the hill at some point. We can. We have to keep perspective, in other words. This could be an uncomfortable couple of days, but we should be okay in the end, right?"

Not right, Mary thought. *Not right at all.* In science class Mary had done a report on the effects of dehydration and she remembered some of the data. They could not make it. They could not go three and a half days without food or water. At least not without water. Not in these temperatures, not if they were going to be working to move the stones. Not even close. In a desert environment, she knew, you could die within hours from a lack of water. But even in cold temperatures a lack of water became a serious concern amazingly fast. You shivered in the cold and burned off liquid. No, they could probably make it without food, but not without water. She was certain of that.

Add to that the fact that they had no blankets, no way to get warmer, and you had a dangerous situation. The air would grow foul, and she didn't even want to think of the bathroom situation. Mr. O'Connell was putting an optimistic spin on things, and while she saw the need to stay positive, she also thought a little more reality might be needed.

"We need to get out of here," she said. "We need to dig. Everyone."

"Except Sam," Ms. Carpenter said.

"Except Sam," Mary agreed. "Everyone except Sam."

"Any questions?" Mr. O'Connell asked softly.

No one spoke. A last tiny tremor rocked them gently and then disappeared into the sea.

Harry's fingers hurt. They hurt a lot. It was long past the point where he wished for gloves, or for a stick of dynamite to blow the rocks out of the doorway. All he knew was that one rock came after another. He took one in his right hand, switched it to his left hand, then passed that to another hand. He'd lost count of how many stones they had moved, but it had to be thousands. And it was all done in the dark. True dark. Like working in the basement of a basement.

"Switch," someone said nearby.

That meant the person at the rear of the line got to have a break. The person who had been resting came to the top of the line and began handing back rocks. Round and round they went. Harry hated it.

"I am sooooo thirsty," Sandy Bellow said.

No one answered her. No one cared.

Then she said, "Are we going to do this, like, forever?"

"Shut up, Sandy," Bob Worm said. "Just keep working."

"But, I mean . . ."

Then Sam Harding moaned. He had done that with increasing frequency, Harry noticed. He was in a lot of pain. His ear had been half-shredded, and his biceps looked like a bear had scraped its claws down his upper arm. One stem on his eyeglasses had broken, too, so they sat on his face like a goofy parody of what people with glasses should look like.

When Sam moaned, everything slowed. Everyone listened. It reminded Harry of the ghost story Azzy had told them before they hopped on the boat. Supposedly Whistling Willy lived on the island. He was a ghost with a cannonball in his guts and an eye that dangled from a thread. Whenever Sam moaned, Harry couldn't help thinking about Whistling Willy.

"What time is it?" Ms. Carpenter asked as the rocks started passing down the line again. "Does anyone know?"

"If I had my cell phone I'd know," Harry said.

No one had a cell phone. That was against the rules of Mr. O'Connell's Outing Club. No electronics.

"Anyone besides Harry know what time it is?" Ms. Carpenter repeated.

"It's only a little after seven," Bob Worm said, catching a glimpse of his watch in the dimming light.

All just voices. All darkness.

Sam lay on the floor, his mind dislocated from his body. At least it felt that way. He listened to the stones dropping on the discard pile, listened to the occasional voices talking about what they were doing. He had trouble staying awake. His arm felt melted into the floor. Or glued there by blood. His head felt foggy and imprecise. As soon as he formed one thought, another chased it away. Mostly he simply stared into the darkness, wondering how this would end.

All stories had to end, he knew. He had watched too many movies not to know that.

But movies weren't life. In real life, you had to take whatever ending came.

△ △ △

A little later they stopped moving stones. It felt late. Bob Worm had a watch, but he couldn't read it now unless he went over to the headlamp. Everyone used cell phones now to tell time, but without cell phones you were left with guesses. Still, it felt like the core of the night, something dark and silent and tight. The air inside the magazine had taken on particles of dust, so that every breath tasted of earth and minerals.

Someone began snoring nearby. Then another person mumbled something in their sleep. He couldn't tell if it was a boy or girl who mumbled. Then Mr. O'Connell – he was pretty sure it was Mr. O'Connell from the deeper sound of the voice – said, "It's early; go back to sleep if you can."

Easier said than done, Sam knew. So he did what he always did to put himself to sleep: He remembered movies. He went through sections of films in slow-motion detail. Scene by scene. Before he made it to the end, sleep came on him again and he felt his body floating up into the darkness, in the cave that they all inhabited, and once, right near sleep, his body jumped at something.

At the quakes, maybe. At the tremors. But his arm lifted a tiny bit and sent a shock wave of pain to his head, and then he fell deep inside himself and did not wake again until he heard them moving rocks, the *ping* of stones oddly comforting as they splattered into the discard pile.

CHAPTER 6

Sandy Bellow stood in front of the tiny slot that still existed in the seaward wall and wondered if they really expected her to slide out through it. The only reason they had picked her, she knew, was that she was the tiniest. No one else stood a chance of fitting through the slot, and she wasn't sure she did, either, but it was worth a try. She understood that. But all she could think about was Azzy and how she had tried to make it outside and how that hadn't ended so tremendously.

"What do you think?" Mr. O'Connell asked her. "You think you can do it?"

"I don't think so."

"Are you game to try it?"

"I don't think so."

She heard someone making a *tsk* sound in disgust. She wanted to turn and say, *Sorry, you try it*, but she controlled herself. Still, she had wanted to tell Bob Worm, Bob Worm especially, the big oaf, that he should try to squeeze through the minuscule little slot if he thought it was so easy.

"Sandy," Ms. Carpenter said, "we could really use some help. It's incredibly important for someone to get out and get water. It's key. Do you think you could do it?"

"I don't think so."

"You need water, too," Mr. O'Connell said, his voice droning on the same thing. "You're going to need it soon, too."

"I know that."

"If we have to dig our way out, it could take another day. Maybe more," Mr. O'Connell said.

Sandy shrugged.

Not that she wanted to be down here any longer. She hated it. She hated everything about it. She had already vowed one thousand times that she would never, ever let anyone talk her into a camping trip again. No way, no how. She couldn't wait to confront Lenny and ask him if she now had "a little Spackle on her tail." *How about now?* she wanted to ask. *What kind of merit badge do I get for this?*

"If your head can go through, you can make it," Ms. Carpenter said. "Maybe you could just give it a small try and see."

"What if things are still falling outside? What if it collapses?"

"It would have collapsed by now if it was going to collapse," Mr. O'Connell said. "It would have given way."

"How do you know that? It could collapse any second. It could collapse and cut me right in half. How do you know that?"

"Why don't you just think about it for a little while?" Ms. Carpenter asked. "Just get your head around the idea. Nobody's going to pressure you."

Bob Worm made a *tsk* sound again.

"Bob . . ." Mr. O'Connell said.

"She's being a jerk," Bob Worm said. "She's always a jerk."

"Bob, that's not helping," Ms. Carpenter said.

"I don't care."

"Bob, stop it," Mr. O'Connell said.

"She could get out and get us water if she just weren't so selfish," Bob said.

"I'm not selfish!" Sandy yelled back at him. "You try it if you think it's so easy."

Then no one said anything. Sam moaned. And then they heard Mary begin moving rocks again. A little more light came in through the slot, and they heard seagulls calling, making baby sounds, Sandy thought, making sounds like people crying.

Harry played the harmonica softly. To his amazement, it sounded good. Or okay, at least. It probably sounded okay because of the echo, but also because it gave everything a little cover. You didn't hear people coughing or sneezing or grumbling because the harmonica covered it all. It felt, honestly, like one of those old cowboy campfires where the young guy pulls out his mouth harp and gives them all a tune.

"That sounds nice," Mary said. She sat close. They all sat close. "It sounds real pretty down here."

Harry nodded. He kept his lips moving on the harmonica.

He didn't play any particular tune. He *couldn't* play any particular tune. But he could play a few notes, and he linked them together fairly well, so that people went along with it. It made his heart hurt a little to play. He thought of them all being trapped down underground, and a harmonica made an awful lot of sense in circumstances like that.

He also thought of Sam. He thought of Sam playing the circle-finger-punch-in-the-arm game on the boat. It made Harry get a little cloudy to look over at Sam and see him still stretched out on the jackets, not moving. Sam was probably the only friend he had. Probably his best friend.

"What songs do you know?" Mr. O'Connell asked. "Can you play any we could sing to? Maybe it would do us good to sing a quiet song."

Harry shrugged. He didn't know any actual songs.

"I think it's just nice to hear the music," Ms. Carpenter said. "Just the sounds."

Harry played and did pretty well, he thought. When he got tired he tapped out the spit from the harmonica and slid it back into his pocket.

"Thank you," Mary said.

Ms. Carpenter said thanks, too. It was surprising how much you missed the music once it was gone, Harry reflected.

"This is bad," Eamon O'Connell whispered to Ursula Carpenter. "This is incredibly bad."

"I know."

"These kids could die down here."

"I know. So could we, Eamon."

"We have to get Sandy to try it."

"Sandy has a mind of her own," Ursula whispered. "She just does."

"She has to see the benefit."

"She's scared, Eamon. We can try to be reasonable with her, but I'm not sure that will work."

He didn't say anything. He backed away slowly and sat on a large boulder that had come loose during the tremors. Ursula wasn't sure what he wanted. Did he want her to follow him, to yell at Sandy, what? It was difficult to know. Truth was, they didn't have any good options. They had been moving rocks for the better part of a day and they still hadn't broken through yet.

"She may not even fit through," Eamon said, continuing the conversation, which meant, Ursula figured, that she should follow him to where he sat. "We don't know that she will. It's awfully narrow."

"Still."

"It's going to be dark again soon."

"The darkness is pretty terrible."

"How do you think Sam is doing?"

She shook her head. Then she realized he couldn't see the motion.

"He's cold and he's in shock. We're going to have to warm him with our bodies tonight."

"I guess so."

"If we can get through, Eamon, we'll be okay. You have the satellite phone out by the tents, right? So one thing at a time. If we get out, everything else will take care of itself."

He put his head in his hands. She sat down beside him. She felt tired and hungry and thirsty. Really thirsty. The cold, too, snuck into your clothing and bones. It wasn't good. The entire situation was pretty horrible.

"It all feels so stupid now," he said, his voice slightly muffled from his hands. "This whole trip."

"You can't do that. You can't look back and say this or that should have happened. You couldn't anticipate an earthquake."

"We just got here," he said. "We hadn't even spent an hour on the island."

"I know."

"Stupid puffins."

She couldn't tell if he meant it as a joke. She smiled and then started to giggle. It was the strange, way-too-tired kind of giggle. She tried to control it, but couldn't. It rattled around her stomach like a squirrel caught in an attic. Her face turned red and bright.

"What's so funny?" Harry Cameron called over from the work line. "Share with all of us."

"Mr. O'Connell," she said, working the words around her silliness, "said puffins are stupid."

No one laughed. It was a case of having to be there, she knew. Or feeling tired in the same way she did. Their lack of comprehension only made her laugh harder.

She was still laughing when Sandy Bellow stepped in front of them.

"I'll try it," Sandy said, her voice straightforward and calm. "I'll try the slot if you still want me to."

"What changed your mind?" Ursula asked.

She hated herself for asking and risking that Sandy might change her mind again, but she couldn't help it.

"I don't want to move more rocks," Sandy said. "If I go out, you have to let me off the work detail."

"That's not negotiable," Eamon said.

Sandy started to walk away, but Ursula called her back.

"Let's try it," Ursula said.

Sandy paused for a moment, then nodded.

Like trying to fit your head in a lion's mouth, thought Bob Worm.

Only he wished it *were* a lion's mouth and Sandy's big head was leaning right into it.

"Ooowwwwww," she said.

She had already said "ooowwwwww" a thousand times.

"Easy does it," Mr. O'Connell said.

He had Sandy's right foot. Bob had her left foot.

Of course he had her foot. If there was lifting to do, call Bob Worm.

"Lean a little more. . . . A little more . . . You're almost clear," Ms. Carpenter said.

"I might get trapped. It's tight. Owwwwwwww."

"If your head makes it, you can get the rest of you through," Ms. Carpenter said.

"Are you sure?" Sandy asked, her voice pinched.

"Sure I'm sure," Ms. Carpenter said. "Lift her a little higher."

Bob locked eyes with Mr. O'Connell and nodded. They lifted her higher.

At least, Bob thought, she didn't weigh much. He gave Sandy that much. In every other way, he thought, she was a waste of space.

"She's making it," Mary Eihorn said.

Everyone stood grouped around. It was late afternoon, Bob knew from checking his watch and from the light that spilled quietly into the underground cavity. He looked at Harry and Mary and wiggled his eyebrows. They didn't see it, or didn't care. Their eyes stayed fixed on Sandy wedging herself slowly through the slot.

"Owwwwwww," Sandy said.

"You're making it," Mary said again.

"It doesn't feel like it. It feels like it's crushing my head."

"A little more," Harry said.

"There are rocks outside here, too," Sandy said, her head nearly out. "Owwwowowww."

"A little higher, Bob," Mr. O'Connell whispered.

Bob lifted. Sandy's head finally went through.

"There you go!" Ms. Carpenter said, her voice all cheerleader-y. "Way to go, Sandy!"

"Owwwwwww."

But now she started moving forward. Bob felt her squiggling through the slot, little by little. In unison with Mr. O'Connell, he lifted her again. Her waist suddenly made it up onto the wall below the slot and she was suspended. Her legs stuck out like a scuba diver's legs sticking out of a shark's mouth.

"Go, go, go, go," Harry started chanting.

Mary didn't chant, Bob noticed. Mary didn't do things like that.

Bob stepped back and watched. The top half of Sandy's body had gone through the slot. Ms. Carpenter motioned to Mr. O'Connell that she wanted to go up to help. Mr. O'Connell motioned to Bob to come help and give Ms. Carpenter a boost up. He did.

"There you go, there you go," Ms. Carpenter said to Sandy, her hand smoothing Sandy down so that her belt and boots went through. "You made it, you made it."

Then Sandy's legs disappeared. A second later her face looked back inside.

"Which way?" she asked.

"Back that way," Ms. Carpenter said, snaking her hand through and pointing. "Go ahead. You can do it. Look how much you've done already. Go ahead, get some water for us. That's the big thing."

"I don't know which way!" Sandy said, crying now. "I'm not some Girl Scout, you know? I don't know which way to go!"

Bob watched Mr. O'Connell squeeze his eyes shut. He was sick of Sandy, Bob knew. Everyone was sick of

Sandy. It was ironic that they all had to depend on her now.

"Down that way," Ms. Carpenter said, trying to be calm, Bob could tell from her tone. Ms. Carpenter pointed emphatically toward the landing point. They were on an island, a spit of land, really, and Bob wanted to shout to Sandy that she wasn't going to get lost. Nobody could get lost on an island this size.

"Sandy, come here. Come down here, where I can whisper to you, okay?" Ms. Carpenter said, her voice going lower so Bob had a hard time hearing. He under-stood she brought her voice down so Sandy would calm down. Sandy's face appeared near the opening, almost as if she were listening through a mail slot. "There. Now take a deep breath. We're depending on you. We are. You have a chance to be a hero. All you need to do is go down to the campsite and bring back some water. Easy, right? Nothing to it. Now slowly get ahold of yourself. You're the only who can do this. . . ."

"It's blowing like crazy out here."

"That may be, but we're not going to worry about that now. We need water. You can also go through Mr.

O'Connell's tent and look for his satellite phone. Is that clear?"

"Which tent?"

"It's right near the wall of the fort. The highest one away from the water, I think. You'll find it. Just be methodical. And we'll need more lights. We'll keep digging, and you can count on us getting out soon. Right now, though, we need water in a bad way. Get the water first, and then everything else will work out. Can you do that?"

Bob Worm assumed Sandy nodded. He couldn't really see.

"You can do this, Sandy," Ms. Carpenter said. "You ready to do this?"

Sandy nodded again, Bob guessed.

"Okay, we'll be right here. Just take your time and move carefully. Walk back the way we came. It isn't far."

"It's getting dark."

"That's okay. There's nothing on the island that can hurt you."

Sandy didn't move away. She didn't say anything, either.

"What, Sandy?" Ms. Carpenter asked.

"Should I look for Azzy?"

"No, not now. No, you just concentrate on getting water, okay?"

Sandy became just a shadow moving away from the slot. Bob lowered Ms. Carpenter.

"Think she'll make it?" Mr. O'Connell asked.

"Sure she will," Ms. Carpenter said.

Bob rubbed his hands against his pant legs. Before he finished, he heard Mary at the pile of stones, already back trying to dig her way out.

CHAPTER 7

Sandy sensed the wind rushing around her and felt confused. It was easy enough for everyone to point and tell her to go this way or that, but those people weren't on this stupid island, standing in the twilight, wind buzzing all around you and the birds making sounds like an insane asylum. Plus, she was alone. It didn't matter if people were inside the magazine, because she was out here, by herself on the fort grounds, trying to remember which way to go.

Down there, Ms. Carpenter had said.

Down where? Sandy now wondered.

She ducked her head lower to keep the wind out of her eyes. The wind made her eyes water. She walked a few paces in the direction that seemed the most likely.

What they didn't know inside was that the landscape had changed. Really changed. The fort had splintered and shattered and stones now littered the ground. They must have fallen off the top tiers and rolled down toward the water. The place didn't even look the same, Sandy reflected, not that she had taken a particularly sharp mental photograph in the first place. A few huge gaps had opened in the earth, places where the rocks underneath had shifted. One of the walls of the fort appeared caved-in and crooked.

She turned sideways in the next gust of wind. It was cold. She had been cold before, down in the magazine, but now it was even colder. She didn't have her gloves or hat. She had left them down below. She stood for a five count waiting for the wind to pass by her.

When the wind let up, she walked downhill. She took her time, worried about falling, worried about things falling *on her*. Her eyes felt watery and dim, and she couldn't tell if she was crying or merely tearing up from the cold and gusts. Either way, it made seeing difficult. Near the edge of the fort, she bellied out and tried to use landmarks to orient herself. It didn't work.

Whatever the fort had looked like before, it didn't look that way anymore. She stopped and looked around. The wind struck her again and she squatted down, made herself small, until it finally let up.

She saw a tent after she walked another fifteen paces. As easy as that. It was pretty close to the water and just around the end of the fort. She walked toward it, feeling more confident. Maybe she would be a hero, she thought. Maybe when it was all said and done, everyone would have to admit that Sandy Bellow was their savior. Maybe Sandy Bellow – she liked thinking this way, she realized – would come out on top, be the one who saved the day. Bob Worm would have to admit it, and that would grind his guts. Everyone would have to admit that a girl, one Ms. Sandy Bellow, had outdone them. She couldn't wait for that.

But those thoughts left her when she came around the end of the fort.

A stone tongue stretched out from the bottom of the fort nearly to the water.

Sandy stopped and didn't move. She didn't know what to do, and her mind felt squirrelly and unhappy.

The wind continued hitting her. She squatted again, trying to get out of the full force of wind, but it was useless. The wall of the fort was gone, scattered like a thousand heavy dice in one throw toward the water.

The tents were under the stones. Crushed. Crushed to smithereens.

Two things came to her mind. The first was, *We would have been dead.* If the tremor had come at night they would have been asleep in their tents and the wall would have fallen on them. The end. It was that obvious. So in some weird and peculiar fateful twist, they were lucky to have been locked in the magazine. She wondered what the group would think about that.

The other thing that came to mind was the simple understanding that everything they had brought, all the food and water, the satellite telephone, everything that meant comfort and any hope of safety of a sort, now lay below five feet of blocked granite. Gone. Obliterated.

And the walls came tumbling down, she thought, her eyes going over the scene in amazement. *Joshua fought the battle of Jericho, Jericho, Jericho / Joshua fought the battle of Jericho, and the walls came tumbling down.*

That was from an old song they sang at summer camp. She sang it softly in a breathy, strained voice, hardly aware of what she was doing. At the same time, she walked slowly toward the pile of rocks. The rocks looked like alligator skin. Like rough, horrible alligator skin that hid a breathing, hideous creature underneath everything. She felt too frightened to go near them.

A gull snapped past in the wind and nearly hit her. She squatted down and felt her bravery slipping away. *Let someone else do it,* she thought. She stood and started back to the slot, back to the magazine. *Let someone else do it,* she thought again, and then the song came back, *the walls came tumbling down,* her mind on fire, her body as cold as it had ever been.

Eamon O'Connell had to force himself to concentrate on the words that Sandy spoke through the slot.

"The wall fell. . . . It crushed everything . . . all our supplies," Sandy said, her head sideways so she could talk through the slot. He was aware of the group circled around him, aware of Sam Harding moaning loudly, barely conscious now, and that sound seemed to drown out everything else.

"What are you saying?" he asked, though some distant, wobbly part of his brain understood very well what she was saying.

They were marooned. That's what she reported.

"Did you check everything?" Ursula asked from a spot underneath the slot. "Sandy, everything?"

"I didn't lift the rocks, if that's what you mean. It's all crushed. I went through the one tent that was still standing. It was Sam's tent, I think. It was just on the edge of the rock slide."

"We need to check everything," Ursula said, speaking calmly, Eamon knew, to keep Sandy from flying off like a crazed kite into the wind.

"It's all over the ground. The rocks are everywhere. We would have been killed if we had been sleeping there."

"Are you sure . . ." Eamon started, trying to get a hold on what had happened.

"Am I sure that we would have been killed? Yes!" Sandy said, her voice rising. "Yes, I'm completely certain."

It was nearly dark behind her head, Eamon saw. He felt a headache kick into a small pinpoint between his eyes.

"Could you go back and check for water?" Harry said. "You said there was a tent. I can't even say how thirsty I am."

"One tent down by the water. The rest are crushed. There's nothing there, you guys. It's all buried."

"Whose tent is that?" Ursula asked the group. "Who camped closest to the water?"

No one answered. *Sam's, probably*, Eamon thought. Just their luck.

"If you could go back and do a full survey," Ursula told Sandy, "that would be an enormous help. There might be a water bottle in the tent. . . . You never know. If you could just go back and take a look . . ."

Eamon saw Sandy shake her head no.

"I went through the tent and there wasn't anything inside it," she said. "I'm not going back down there by myself."

Then she started crawling back through the slot. It annoyed him to see her squeezing through, her panicked face grinding in pantomime to her body as she wriggled to rejoin them. He felt exhausted watching her.

Bob Worm stepped forward and helped Sandy slide down the wall. She said *owwwwww, owwwww, owwwwww* half a dozen times. Then she was back among the fold. Eamon had to walk away from her to gain his composure. *If only one person could fit through the slot, why did it have to be Sandy?* he wondered.

He sat on the rock he had come to think of as his place. Funny, but each of them had adopted a space in the dim interior. His space was a rock the size of a footstool that allowed him to sit with his back against the stone wall. He felt thirsty and angry and testy. It would be dark in under an hour, he knew. Even if he could talk Sandy into going out again – which he doubted – she would be useless in reconnoitering the situation. It was not even worth considering. He didn't even know if she had really bothered to go through the standing tent.

"We're in a pickle," Harry Cameron said, coming over.

Harry always found a way to step away from removing rocks from the entrance, Eamon noted. He was a master at goldbricking. Harry always made it seem that whatever else needed doing was more pressing than the job at hand, but his real trick was escaping down and dirty labor.

"I know that, Harry," Eamon said, doing his best to keep his voice even.

"No food, no water. That boat guy won't be back for a couple days anyway."

"I know," Eamon repeated.

"Wow," Harry said. "I'm dead thirsty already. I've never been this thirsty."

"I'm sorry about that."

"What's our plan?"

"Oh, I don't know. Maybe I'll get hungry enough to eat through the rocks."

"Whoa, sorry."

"I don't have a plan," Eamon said, checking his sarcasm. "Sorry. Wish I did. If I had a plan, I'd let you know."

"Just asking."

"The plan was to get Sandy out so she could bring back food and water."

"Okay."

Sam moaned loudly. He sounded like a ghost. His voice seemed to penetrate the walls. Eamon took a deep breath.

"Eventually," he said, letting his voice go loud enough so anyone could listen, "someone will come to find us. That's not even an issue. A whole group of kids can't go missing without an alarm being raised."

"That's true," Harry agreed. "We have that going for us."

Sandy came over and stood next to Harry.

"It was really scary out there," she said.

"I bet," Eamon said.

"You still could have searched a little more," Harry said. "At least checked the tent you talked about seeing. Someone might have kept a water bottle in there."

"You go do it if you're so sure it's so easy," Sandy said scornfully. "You try it."

"Thanks anyway, Sandy," Eamon said, realizing from her words that she hadn't bothered to search the tent properly. "At least we know more than we did."

Then Eamon felt something in the chamber change. A sound stopped. At first he thought it was Sam leaving off moaning for a moment, but that wasn't it. It was something deeper, something that had been going along at the edge of his hearing longer than he could recall. He pushed himself up. For the briefest instant, he worried another tremor had shaken the room. But that wasn't it. It was something vaguely rhythmic that had now withdrawn. The fading light made it difficult to see, but then he sensed Ursula stepping across the interior.

"There," he heard Mary say, her voice resolute and strong. "We're through. I can see out."

Eamon felt new, fresh air coming in from the entrance side. Mary, good Mary, had punched through at last.

Dimly, Sam heard people talking. He could no longer be sure whether people talked in his dream, or talked to him in reality. That was interesting. His arm, for reasons he couldn't fully understand, felt like a doorway that he could pass through backward or forward, upward or downward, into dreaming or into consciousness. He wondered, frankly, how he had gotten along so well and so long without his revolving-door arm. Yes, it was a strange thing to have. It was all confusing, no question. Moans came out of his mouth at unexpected moments, moments he couldn't do a thing about, and sometimes he heard them from a distance, like a foghorn, and other times he knew they squeezed out of his own body.

Interesting. It was all very interesting.

"We're going to carry you out," Mr. O'Connell said suddenly, his mouth close by. "We're going to get you out of here. You strong enough for that?"

Sam nodded. Then he realized he needed to speak. But instead of words, the moan came out. It sounded like the croak of a bullfrog.

"The hole isn't that big, so we're going to have to drag you a little. But we need to get out of here," Mr. O'Connell said. "We're going to get a fire going and try to get some food heated up and you'll feel a lot better then, okay?"

Sam moaned again. He didn't want to moan, but he couldn't help it.

"What food?" he heard someone ask nearby. It was a girl's voice, maybe Sandy's.

Sam didn't hear the answer.

Then a bunch of arms lifted him. It was awkward, too, because he kept falling through the arms and drooping down. Once, he felt his butt drag along the ground and dirt went down the back of his pants. They tilted him up and he felt cold air pushing on him. Very cold air. But it was fresh air, too, not bad, and then he was outside and he could see the stars and it was night.

"Okay, okay, let's put him down."

Sam had lost track of who was speaking when. Voices popped at him from different compass points, and it was all quite intriguing, really, but difficult to understand, too.

He smelled woodsmoke. Just a little.

"We need to keep him warm," someone said close to his head.

Then he saw the fire. It was not big, not big at all, and it looked peculiarly orange. People moved around its perimeter. They looked like dark goblins, shaded and indistinct.

Someone bent close to his ear and whispered.

"Just hold on," the person said.

It was a woman. But she seemed to speak from some place up in the sky and he was not sure whether to listen to her or not. It was possible the voice belonged to a fury, a banshee who came to carry his soul away. He had heard of such things. He had heard of souls being tricked into leaving their hosts and he was unsure if that's what was happening to him.

Thirsty, he tried to say.

But his lips were glued shut by dirt and dust. He managed to moan softly, but that did not bring him water. Water, he decided, was what he really wanted.

Mary squatted close to the fire. People came and went, carrying back anything they could find to burn. She nursed the fire carefully. She did not want to let it die.

Mary had been able to start a fire using some dried-out sticks with pinecones and needles. It smelled good. Mary fed the fire slowly, not rushing it. Her father had taught her how to make a fire, and she was glad for the knowledge.

After instructing everyone to stay clear of their landing site, Mr. O'Connell and Ms. Carpenter had gone off to search for food and water among the rubble of the collapsed fort. Everyone else they assigned to wood duty, but that didn't mean those people actually did much. Mary had been designated fire guardian. Or fire warden. It was said as a joke, but she didn't take it that way. They needed a fire. And they needed water.

"Here," Sandy said and dropped three tiny sticks into the woodpile beside the growing flames.

Sandy had not left the light of the fire, Mary knew.

"We need more than that," Mary said flatly. "We need to keep this going."

"Why don't you go find some, then?" Sandy asked, squatting next to the fire.

"I'm responsible for the fire. Do you know how to build and maintain a fire?"

Sandy didn't say anything. She held her hands out to the fire instead.

"We need more wood, Sandy. Please keep working."

Sandy didn't move.

Mary was totally fed up with Sandy. When Bob

Worm came back with a decent armful of wood, Mary asked him to take Sandy with him. He shook his head immediately, but then met Mary's eyes and shrugged. Bob Worm, Mary decided, was okay.

Sandy and Bob disappeared into the darkness. Harry Cameron came back with half a lobster pot. The wood was dry and thin and she told him to put it on the fire carefully. He didn't bother being careful and the fire bent sideways when he tossed it on and looked like it wanted to go out. Then it started catching again. It took the struts of the lobster pot and burned brightly for the first time. The strings holding the struts together burned with bright, friendly sizzles.

"Decent," Harry said.

He held his hands out to the fire. It was late, late night. Or early morning. Mary smelled the sea everywhere. She could not seem to get herself fully oriented.

"Once we get a good bed of coals, we'll be okay. I just want to make sure until then," Mary said.

"No problem. Any word from Mr. Puffin?"

Harry said it with a mocking tone. She couldn't blame him.

"No, not yet."

"If we don't get water, man, we're up a creek."

"Everything on the island is going to be salty. You can't drink salt water."

"I know. That wall smashed our camp."

Mary didn't say anything. What was there to say? Or rather, what wasn't there to say? Any subject you brought up led to an uncomfortable topic. Better to remain silent. Falling rocks had pummeled the food and water. Mary remembered the water containers and she remembered how they had arranged them next to the fort wall. They had brought three plastic jugs, all of them as large as an average lampshade. It was plenty of water, probably too much, even, but she imagined Mr. Puffin wanted to err on the side of caution. Ironic. The plastic containers, all with red carrying handles, had been made of the same type of plastic used to make plastic jugs of milk. Perfectly fine, she acknowledged, until an enormous rock landed on it. The water jugs had exploded like old eggs, she imagined. The food lay buried next to it.

She was still thinking of the water and the food when Harry pulled out his harmonica. He didn't play it, but simply ran his lips over the holes in a quick trill, then put the harmonica back in his pocket.

"How long have you played?" she asked.

"Not long. A month or two."

"It's nice that you can have music whenever you want."

He shrugged. Then she saw Ms. Carpenter and Mr. O'Connell coming toward the fire. She looked at their faces, then at their hands. Their faces told the story, then had it repeated by their empty hands. Nothing. They had found nothing. And they were on an island without water, without food, without a boat, with no means to contact anyone, with no dependable shelter. Marooned, that's what they were, she realized. She had always thought of that happening in some warm, tropical place, mostly to pirates or people from long ago, but no, it had happened to her. In Maine. Outside of Portland. On the busiest shopping weekend of the year.

PART THREE

MAROONED

SURVIVAL TIP #3

Follow several logical steps if you are marooned on an island. First, decide that you are going to do whatever it takes to survive. You're going to have to set aside just about every custom and preference you have if you're going to live for more than a few days on a deserted island. Second, identify a clean source of freshwater. Safe drinking water is your first priority. If you don't have clean, safe drinking water within three to four days, you'll die. The farther inland you go, the more likely you are to find freshwater. Finally, let other people know where you are. Whether that's with a signal fire, or by placing rocks in a large HELP pattern on the beach, figure out ways to let planes and ships know you are in distress.

CHAPTER 8

Bertie Smith had his hands in a sink of dishwater when his heart began to give way. It didn't go all at once, but staggered him sufficiently that he was able to take two steps to his kitchen table and swing his hindquarter around and sit in his usual chair. His chest rocked him with pain. A tiny electric bolt in his head wondered if he wasn't suffering something life-threatening, but his instinctual determination, earned through sixty-seven years of lobstering and roaming the bays beyond Portland, had left him with a hard, staunch character. He didn't believe in illness.

But it came anyway and he put his head down on the kitchen table, his forearm sticking to one of the plastic place mats his daughter had brought last Christmas during her annual visit from Indiana. The place mats had pictures of lobster boats and lobster pots, and Bertie, with his head down next to the empty potato bowl and the dribbles of gravy he hadn't yet cleaned up, found it almost funny that he should feel such a pain in his chest while his eyes stayed riveted to the lobster boat picture. A nice-looking boat, he admitted. Its name wasn't visible from the camera angle, but he had seen a boat like that once, from up in Halifax, Nova Scotia, and he recalled admiring it. So that's what he felt when the final tremor took him.

He *did* think of the kids out on the island, but what good was that? he wondered. He knew in his final moments that he wasn't going to be the one to fetch them. That was someone else's job now, and he wished there was something he could do or say to make it better, or to inform someone, but he couldn't even open his mouth to begin. They might have to put in a few days extra but someone would eventually get them. He wanted to tell Barney, a man he'd known since boyhood, a fellow with a boat who could have picked them up dandy, but it was too late for that. The wall phone looked to be a thousand miles away and the lobster boat on the place mat had begun to carry him out to pull his last pots.

Bob Worm watched light come across the ocean. It wasn't strong and it didn't warm him, but he was still grateful for it. He looked around the fire, trying to see who else was awake. Hard to say. People snored. Even girls snored, which was news to him. He hadn't known girls did that. His dad was the big snore king at his house. But Sandy and even Ms. Carpenter brought the old crosscut saw back and forth against a block of maple and let it rip. Mary, not so much.

He reached down and put more wood on the fire. It was his job to do. He had first watch.

Dew had pushed the fire lower. He had to squat down and blow into it to get it hotter. It wasn't as easy to keep a fire going as you thought. Burn dry wood in a stove, no problem. But a campfire took a ton of fuel and pushed most of the heat into the ground. Bob knew that. He felt as though he had always known that. Every spring he went to his uncle John's sugar bush and helped boil off the syrup. They used stacks of pine slabs on that chore. It was funny how things you didn't know you had learned along the way came back to help you when you didn't expect it.

When the fire became more secure, he lifted back up and resumed his position. He was hungry and he was mad thirsty. Insanely thirsty. He tried to think back and remember his last drink of water. *Before the boat ride over,* he thought. That was his last drink. He couldn't remember consuming anything after that, anyway, and so using that as a fixed time he estimated it had been a day and a half. A little longer, maybe. They had arrived on Friday afternoon, been trapped all day Saturday, and now it was Sunday morning.

The lobster guy was coming back in two and a half days. They needed water before that. That was simple to understand.

He heard Sam moan from inside the tent. They had brought the tent around – it was Sam's tent anyway – and listened while the wind made the tent chatter and snap. The kid wasn't doing great. Bob liked Sam and was sorry to see his injuries, but the kid seemed to live on a different island now. He was with them, but he was also apart. The sick went to a different country, his dad always said. Bob sort of knew what he meant now.

Bob found himself thinking of his dad a lot in this early dawn. He couldn't say why. His dad was not a great guy in every way, no illusions about that, but still, still, he had his moments. His dad was good at making Sunday breakfast, for instance: orange juice, waffles if you wanted, and bacon and sausage. Eggs always. His dad liked to read the Sunday papers, look at the car ads, check the high school football scores. Even when he was deep in the paper, his dad was always willing to pop to the stove and heat something up, microwave a cinnamon roll or get some fresh strawberry jam for your toast. It was as if he counted on Sunday breakfast making up for a ton of not being around, making up for the shouting and the chores. Bob Worm didn't know what to think about it all, but he liked remembering Sunday breakfast with his dad. He liked thinking about that a lot.

He was still thinking about his dad and Sunday breakfast when Mr. O'Connell woke up, rubbed his face, then stood and came around the fire. Mr. O'Connell looked horrible. Dirt lined the creases of his forehead and his nails and hands looked like badger claws. Bob Worm wondered if he looked as bad as Mr. O'Connell did. Probably so.

"How's it going, Bob?" Mr. O'Connell asked, squatting near and holding his hands out. "You're keeping the fire going, I see."

"We're getting low on wood."

"We'll get people moving on it when they wake up. There should be plenty around. Plenty of driftwood."

"Okay."

"You thirsty?"

Bob nodded.

"They say if you suck on a pebble sometimes it helps. I want to look around and see if the dew can provide us with some water. I want to take a good look at the tents and everything. We couldn't make out much last night."

"The fire is good."

"A fire helps morale," Mr. O'Connell said. "Even if we weren't so cold, I'd make us build a fire. Gives everyone a center."

"We need water."

"I know. I'm trying to remember my high school chemistry about salt content in seawater. I think it's around thirty percent by volume. Something like that. I don't know how we desalinate it."

"If we could catch some gulls, we could drink bird blood."

Mr. O'Connell looked at him. Then he smiled.

"Whoa. You've watched too many zombie shows. Not sure we're there yet, Bob, but I'll keep it in mind. Captain Bertie will be back day after tomorrow."

"In the afternoon?"

Mr. O'Connell nodded. He threw another piece of wood on the fire.

"Does anyone expect to hear from us?"

Mr. O'Connell looked a little uncomfortable about the question. He cleared his throat and stood.

"I'll be honest, Bob. I made a big deal of making sure we had no electronics on the trip. Well, you heard my lectures on the topic. No video games, no movies, no anything. I told my wife I wouldn't call on the satellite phone unless it was an emergency. Big, brave *Mr. Puffin.* Now I can't call, and I've arranged it so she won't call. Circumstances, Bob. See how they work into the situation?"

Bob nodded. He was thinking it was pretty cool that Mr. O'Connell had been honest with him. He was also thinking it was pretty cool that Mr. O'Connell was being honest with himself.

"I'm going to scout around," Mr. O'Connell said, stretching again. "Keep the fire going. Get people to collect wood when they wake up."

"Okay."

Mr. O'Connell scanned the area before he took off.

"We'd be warmer inside, but I'm not willing to risk it again," he said.

"It was pretty crazy in there."

Bob felt Mr. O'Connell touch him on the shoulder, then heard him walk off. *Mr. Puffin.* Bob picked up a half-dozen pieces of wood and fed them to the fire.

Mary felt wobbly and light-headed. Dehydration, she knew. She carried an armful of wood back toward the fire but had to stop twice to regain her energy. It drained her to put the wood down, rest, then pick it up again. She might have carried lighter loads and made more trips, but that didn't seem so great, either. Everything came down to energy in, energy out, water in, water out. She had known that intellectually before, but she had never really understood it in her gut.

She was hungry, too. Very hungry. Her insides felt like a dozen birds fluttering.

Use your head, she kept thinking. That phrase rolled in and out of her mind, but never entirely left it. Her mother had always said that to her. *Use your head*. She said that life didn't depend on fancy tools, but on your mind. On your attitude. If you met challenges directly, made reasoned decisions, then your chances improved exponentially. You had to think before you acted.

But if you couldn't find water, you couldn't find water. And you couldn't survive. That was the long and short of it, she knew.

She was glad to make it back to the fire and to dump the wood from her arms. She was glad to get out of her own head, too.

"Where is everyone?" she asked Harry Cameron, who was on fire duty for the time being. It was still early morning, the sun a few feet above the horizon line.

"Collecting wood," Harry said, waving at the land around him. "Most of the wood is down by the water."

"I know," Mary said. "I just came from there."

"Ms. Carpenter was in with Sam. He's not doing so great."

"Is he worse?"

"He needs water and food. They're worried about him. Really worried."

"It all comes down to water," Mary said.

"Do you feel light-headed?"

Mary nodded.

"I do, too. Mr. Puffin has a headache and his lips look cracked. It's like we're on a desert island, which is crazy because we're up here in Maine."

"I know. It is crazy."

"If it would rain or snow, we'd be okay. But it's completely sunny."

"It's cold, though. The temperature is dropping."

"When we have enough wood, Mr. Puffin wants us to build a HELP sign with rocks. He thinks someone might see it from the air."

"We can't expend too much energy, though," Mary said. "That will burn up water faster than anything."

"I'm just saying what he said."

She didn't speak for a minute or more. She knew she should go back and get more wood, but she had no energy. In time the others came back, all of them carrying wood. They dropped the wood into a pile and didn't move away. Mr. O'Connell was the last one back. Harry had been right, Mary saw: Mr. O'Connell looked shaky and weak.

"Come on, everyone, please give me your attention," Mr. O'Connell asked. "Can you please just hold on for a second?"

Not many people were speaking anyway, Mary thought. Mr. O'Connell stepped close to the fire and held out his hands. He started to speak twice before he finally gained sufficient saliva to begin.

"Here are our options as I see them," Mr. O'Connell

said. "No matter what, we need to stay positive. Everyone agrees on that, right?"

Mary saw people nod.

"Nobody expected this," he continued. "No one planned for anything like this. Our equipment is buried under the rocks. Our food is buried, too. Ms. Carpenter and I studied the likelihood of digging it out and we don't think the chances are very good. The rocks are extremely heavy, for one thing, and the wall above looks to be unstable. I'm not entirely sure we could get to the supplies, and I think it's too dangerous to try in any case."

Mary looked around the group. Everyone had come to the same conclusion. Harry put a few more pieces of wood onto the fire.

"Ms. Carpenter and I also discussed the possibility of moving back into the magazine in order to be out of the wind. I'm sure you all considered that might be a good thing to do, but again, we're worried about the stability of the structure. If another tremor comes, we don't want to be trapped inside. I think we all agree on that."

"Then what *are* we going to do?" Sandy asked, her voice whiny and plaintive. "All you're saying is what we can't do. How about what we *can* do?"

Mary watched Mr. O'Connell turn his gaze on Sandy. Mr. Puffin suddenly looked like Mr. Vulture. It was easy to see he didn't care for Sandy. Mary watched him slowly get a grip on his anger.

"We're going to collect dew for water," Mr. O'Connell said. "If you have a cotton T-shirt, we're going to need it. Or even a bandanna. We're going to drag the grass with our T-shirts, then wring them out into the one drinking bottle we have with us. It will be a slow, tedious process, but it's a known survival technique."

"What about food?" Bob Worm asked.

"We can probably survive without food, but the ocean is our best chance of finding something. We need everyone to be vigilant. Also, we need to come up with a signaling system so that if someone does come by in a boat or a plane, we'll be noticed. Who wants to be on that team?"

No one raised a hand.

Ms. Carpenter stepped forward and pointed to Bob, Harry, and Mary. That left Sandy alone with Mr. O'Connell.

"Sandy, you're on fire duty. Keep it going, but don't use more wood than necessary. I'm going to start dragging the grass for dew."

"Is it too early?" Harry asked.

"Maybe it will be more frost than dew, but it might work. It's our one source of water. If it works, we'll be in better shape."

A cold wind blew across the top of the island. Mary turned to be out of it. The fire flickered and made a sound like a piece of sail coming free in a breeze.

CHAPTER 9

Bob Worm found the boat. It was weird to spot it because he realized that he had walked past it a dozen times without picking it out. Someone had covered it with a camouflage tarp, and the pattern blended surprisingly well. It resembled rocks and sand and a bunch of puckerbush, and even after he saw it he had to step closer to make sure his eyes weren't playing tricks on him.

But no, it was a boat. It looked to be old as a donkey, as his aunt Bertha would have said, but it was a boat. Fourteen footer, he guessed, a skiff. Or dory. Something to deliver goods back and forth to the mainland or to a boat at anchor. He started to laugh when he saw it.

"Hey," he yelled, but was surprised to discover his voice was merely a croak. He had to bend over, get a little spit in his mouth, then try it again.

"Hey, over here! A boat!"

He saw Ms. Carpenter look up. She had them writing out HELP on the beach closest to the mainland. They had a bunch of white rocks already forming the *H* and *E* and part of the *L*.

"A boat," he said. "I just found a boat."

He pointed. One after another, they stood and scrambled toward him.

"I never even saw it!" Mary exclaimed. "It was right under our noses."

"It's a boat!" Harry said. "An actual boat."

"Is it in good shape?" Ms. Carpenter asked. "Let's pull the tarp back. Is it okay?"

Bob grabbed one end of the tarp and walked it backward along the side of the boat. The tarp didn't want to come off. It stuck where the cold had trapped it against the wooden bottom and plants had grown through it and anchored it to the spot. It made a sound like snaps coming loose, but Bob kept pulling, feeling pretty excited. The tarp was in rough shape.

"Wow," Harry said when Bob had the tarp pretty far back. "That's an old boat."

Bob saw it, too. It was an old wooden rowboat. Heavy as anything, Bob guessed. Probably dense and partially waterlogged already. Bob studied the rotted keel, no longer feeling the same sense of triumph he had a moment before. Yes, it was a boat, he saw, but it was hard to say if it was reliable.

"Do you think it's any good?" Mary asked. "Do you think it's seaworthy?"

"It's not very far to the mainland," Harry said. "Probably a mile, maybe."

"That is a long way to row," Ms. Carpenter said, her eyes running up and down the boat. "Does anyone see any oars? Can we lift it up and look underneath?"

Bob knew who was going to do the lifting. It was the same old story. This time, though, he didn't mind. They all arranged themselves along one edge and hoisted. Something gooey followed the boat up. *Mushrooms*, Bob thought. The wood on the gunwale he held felt mushy and soft. The boat appeared in worse shape than he had thought.

But the oars were there. They looked much younger and better than the rest of the vessel.

"Gee, I don't know," Ms. Carpenter said. "What do you guys think?"

"It's not great," Harry said.

"I'll go get Mr. O'Connell," Mary said, turning to jog off. "He'll want to see this."

"It's been out in the weather for years, looks like," Ms. Carpenter said. "But it might be solid enough to make it to the mainland. That tarp was shot a long time ago."

"I don't think the oarlocks will hold," Bob said. "Let's drop it back down."

They counted to three and dropped it. It almost nipped Harry's toes, but he jumped backward just in time.

Mr. O'Connell arrived a few minutes later with Mary.

"What do you think?" Ms. Carpenter asked after they had repeated the process of lifting it and showing it to Mr. O'Connell.

"It's hard to say, isn't it?" he asked. "I think we should drag it down to the water and check it out. We can float it and see if it holds or starts to leak right away."

"I'm not sure it's seaworthy," Ms. Carpenter said.

"Well, I guess we won't know until we try it. If it can carry one of us to the mainland, then that solves a lot of problems."

Then they flipped the boat. It was easier said than done. When they dragged it off a few paces, they discovered a dried carcass underneath it. The carcass was so dry and so flattened that it was difficult to say what kind of animal it had been. *Fox*, Bob thought. *Or maybe a cat or raccoon.* He didn't inspect it too closely.

Luckily, the boat wasn't far from the water. Still, it reminded Bob of a time when he and his dad had lifted a refrigerator up a set of basement stairs without a hand truck. Lift, shove, rest. Lift, shove, rest. The boat felt watery and soft and a couple times Bob wondered if they weren't going to peel the bottom right off it.

But it made it. They shoved the nose of the boat into the water and it suddenly lifted and was no longer an unwieldy, heavy thing.

"Well, at least it floats," Mary said when they slowly turned it around on the water so that the prow faced them. "That's a start."

"It might leak a little until the joints swell," Mr. Puffin said, examining the interior. "That's the way it is with these old wooden boats."

"Do you really think someone should chance it?" Bob asked. "If you get halfway to the mainland and it starts to leak big-time, you're a dead man."

"We're in a bit of a pickle, in case you didn't notice," Mr. Puffin said offhandedly, his eyes still running back and forth over the boat. "I'm worried about Sam. He needs medical attention and he needs water and food. We all do."

"Still," Bob said.

"If the boat floats, it's doable," Ms. Carpenter said. "I rowed in college. We did miles at a time."

But not in a big, heavy tub, Bob thought, his mind trying to figure the odds. This boat, even when it was freshly minted, wasn't cut out for long voyages. He imagined people might have made it over to the mainland on a soft summer day, but this was no soft summer day, that was for sure.

"Let's let it sit for a while and see how it does," Mr. Puffin said. "If it takes on water, then we'll have that as information. Grab some of that rope, would you, Mary?"

Mary grabbed a length of rope. It was nylon rope, yellow and red strands intertwined, one of a thousand pieces around the island's shoreline. The rope came off lobster pots and washed around, jamming propellers and getting tangled on everything. Eventually, it washed up on the island, frayed and bleached. That was supposed to be a large part of the reason for visiting the island in the first place, Bob recalled. They were going to clean off nesting sites for puffins. That plan seemed like something from a million years ago.

But at least they had plenty of rope. Bob helped Mr. Puffin tie the boat off and attach the free end to a huge metal ring that had been cemented into a granite block. The boat rode comfortably on its leash, bobbing and occasionally nudging forward to click softly against the rocky shore. When Bob looked inside the boat, he saw that it had taken on water, definitely, but it wasn't a drastic situation. It looked like the wood had become spongy and soft, but maybe it had one more trip in it.

"Okay, that's pretty good," Mr. Puffin said. "That's a little ray of hope right there, isn't it? Now, if I can make some water out of dew, we'll be in business."

"This is intense," Harry said, following Mr. Puffin back. "I mean it. This is way intense."

Bob fell in behind them. It *was* intense, Bob thought. He made a quick detour and went back to look at the carcass they had unearthed by lifting the boat. *A fox*, he thought. He was pretty sure it had been a fox.

Eamon dragged his T-shirt over the grass at the foot of the fort. Mary and Sandy and Harry walked higher up on the hillside, their T-shirts dragging behind them, too. It was working. To his amazement, it was working, and he felt a glimmer of pride in remembering this small survival tip from a weekend Scouting trip he had taken when he was ten.

The trick was to take your T-shirt, twist one end and turn it into a little ghost, tie a rope around the knotted head, then drag the whole contraption behind you as you walked. A ghost or a small dog. If you walked slowly and carefully, the T-shirt absorbed the dew, then you could squeeze the extra water into a drinking vessel, and voilà, survival. It was slow, tedious work, and you had to be careful not to drag the T-shirt ghost through poisonous weeds, but little by little you gathered water. Eamon felt confident that later, when the hard frost settled on the island, they would harvest more water faster. Now that they knew the trick, they could have a team harvesting all night long if need be. Dehydration, remarkably, was no longer a serious threat.

When he judged his T-shirt to be well soaked, he walked to the spilling station, where Ursula kept the Nalgene bottle. She held a bandanna over the mouth of the vessel as a filter. Eamon squeezed the water into the cavity she had poked into the mouth of the cloth and watched a thin trickle of water drip down into the bottle.

"Not bad," Ursula said. "I took the first drink up to Sam. He wouldn't wake up so I gave him a little, just dripped it into his mouth, but I worried he'd choke."

Eamon nodded. Sam was the issue. Sam was the very big issue.

"Let's try to keep count and go in rotation so that everyone gets a fair portion. You can adjust for body size, but everyone needs some right away."

"Agreed."

Eamon started to head off when Ursula asked him to wait a moment.

"I think I should take the boat," she said when he came back toward her. "It's still floating."

"It's taken on a lot of water."

"I know. But I could bail, too. We have that rusty paint can, and we could use it as a bailer. I could go alone. We wouldn't be risking two lives."

"We only have to make it till Tuesday. It's Sunday already."

"I know, but I don't think Sam can last," she said, her voice going low as Sandy came up with her T-shirt of frost. Sandy, to her credit, Eamon thought, actually performed the task well and didn't complain for a change. She went off to keep reloading her T-shirt with water.

When Sandy left, Ursula continued.

"If I can make it across, Sam will have medical attention a day and a half earlier. It might be the difference."

"You mean life and death? You really think so?"

Ursula shrugged.

"It seems like it. I'm not a doctor, but his pulse seems light and irregular. He hasn't eaten and has had only a little water. We've made him as comfortable as possible, but he's probably cold. Whatever fell on him almost scraped his ear off. Maybe it injured his head, too."

Eamon nodded. She had just outlined his own thinking, too.

"If anybody goes, I'll go," he said. "I'm the one who brought us here; I'm the one who should assume the risk."

"But I'm a better rower. I was a great rower in college, Eamon. I'm really good at it, and I'm really strong."

"I don't like it."

"If the boat floats through the night and the sea is calm tomorrow, I want to try it. We owe it to Sam."

"True, but it won't help Sam if you are midway to the mainland and the boat sinks."

"I agree. But we're going to be careful and check it out first."

She stopped talking. Harry came up with his T-shirt and squeezed its moisture into the bottle. His addition gave them a half bottle. That was one and a half bottles in maybe an hour, an hour and a half, Eamon calculated. Not much, but enough to get them through. The frost, after the sun went down, might yield better results.

"Let's look at it in the morning," Eamon said. "Let's see how the boat does during the night."

She nodded. He went off to drag his T-shirt through the grass. It was a cold, bright late afternoon.

Sandy sat on the beach and thought about the mall. Actually, it didn't feel as though she thought about the mall as much as the mall invaded her consciousness. She pictured the warm air coming out of the vents; the sunglasses shop where the cute boy, Victor, worked and let her try on as many pairs as she liked; the clothing outlet with all the flashy, beautiful things and the free vials of perfume; Mrs. Johnson, who liked to gossip as she folded things; and the food court, where Sandy could slowly work her way around from Panda Pasta to Pizza Express to Oriental Chaos. Yes, she missed the mall. She missed its orderly presence, its comfort, its warm, soothing environment. She promised herself that she would never, ever come camping again. Not for any reason. Not for anyone.

She was still sitting there when Mary came by and told her they still needed more wood for the fire.

"I'm resting," Sandy said.

She didn't really want to work, but more than that, she didn't want to leave her daydream of the mall.

"We need wood," Mary repeated.

"Does it look like my ears fell off?"

"If you heard me, why don't you do what you're asked?"

"Because you are not the queen of England."

"I don't need to be the queen of England to ask you to do your share."

"Get over yourself, Mary."

Sandy didn't even bother looking at Mary. She kept her eyes on the ocean and her brain on the mall. She heard Mary give a little huff of exasperation, then stalk off. Sandy didn't care. If you didn't care, it usually didn't matter what other people did. She had discovered that a long time ago.

Mr. Puffin came by a little later and sat down beside her. Sandy didn't acknowledge him because she knew he came to give her the *talk*. Teachers loved to give you the talk, she knew. She had heard it plenty of times and Mr. Puffin didn't hold out much promise of originality. She wondered what he would say if she turned the tables and tried to lecture him about responsibility.

"So, Mary said you two had a disagreement about collecting wood," Mr. Puffin started. "Is that fair to say?"

"Not really."

"Why not?"

"Because I didn't disagree. I just said I was resting."

"But other people are working. You must be able to see how it bothers people to see you sitting here while they are working."

"If they need a rest, they should stop and take it. I won't tell them they have to keep going."

"But we all have to pitch in."

"I'm the one who climbed through the window, remember? I'm the one who risked her life."

"I wouldn't say you risked your life by doing that."

"Well, you weren't the one who had to squeeze through that little slot, were you?"

She didn't look at him, but she could feel his slow burn. It almost made her laugh. Why didn't other people know what she knew? All you had to do was say no, calmly and surely, and people couldn't do much about it.

"Listen, I'm on your side, Sandy. I'm trying to make you understand why people may sometimes have a hard time with you."

"Gee, thanks."

"You're being sarcastic. I'm being sincere."

"I don't want your sincerity. Thanks, but no thanks."

He didn't say anything, but she heard him breathing harder.

"You've got a long life ahead of you," Mr. Puffin said, his voice a little tattered with emotion. "It's going to be difficult if you don't mend your ways."

"You mean so I can be a person like you who leads a bunch of kids onto an island and gets them in this situation? If I change, I can be like you?"

He didn't say anything. She felt him boiling. People boiled easier than you might guess if you knew how to do it.

"I'll ignore that remark," he said.

She didn't reply.

"So it's your position that you should sit and do nothing while other people work? Is that what you're saying?"

"Is that what I said?"

"It's what you imply."

"Take it how you want to."

"Sandy, quit being so unreasonable."

"People always say you're unreasonable if you don't do what they want you to do."

"What's that supposed to mean?"

She shrugged. For a second, she imagined fast food – the steel-colored scooper going through a new pile of fries. Then salt. Then a blat of ketchup next to it. That's what she wanted to think about.

She didn't say anything else. Mr. Puffin finally got the message.

After his departure, it took her a few minutes to regain her mental map of the mall. She liked going into the candle store. Nothing made her happier than the scent of a bunch of candles. Some people hated it, but not her. She thought candles smelled better than just about anything.

CHAPTER 10

Ursula pushed the boat off the rocky shore and climbed nimbly onto the rowing bench. It was early morning, the water as calm as a puddle. Gulls sang and reeled above her. The grassy slope rising up to the fort had been coated white by frost. It was a cold morning, but calm, and Ursula imagined making the crossing nearly before the others had come fully awake.

She loved to row, and she was good at it. She had rowed crew in college. The rowboat beneath her now was a far cry from a streamlined skull, but rowing was rowing in some sense. The skiff felt leaden and bogged in the water, but when she leaned into the oars the boat responded reasonably well.

Eamon, she understood, would be furious with her. She knew that. But he would insist on rowing the passage himself, playing the senior teacher role, or at the very least the guy role, and she hated that stuff. Given her skill with oars, it made sense for her to attempt the crossing. She hoped it would not be a big deal in any case.

When she pulled on the oars again she checked the oarlocks. Specifically, she checked to see if the oarlocks were going to hold. Everything about the boat felt like a damp paper bag, soggy and ready to pull apart given any pressure, but at least it cut through the first tiny chop successfully. The oarlocks – the seats for the oars, the metal posthole where you slid the metal bracket into it – looked as though they could pull out anytime.

What she worried about was the halfway point.

It was like the old joke-riddle: *How far can you go into the woods?*

Answer: *Halfway.*

At some point, Ursula understood, she would have to make a decision to go for it or to turn back. She promised herself that she would be coolly clinical about the decision. Now was not the time for heroics or shoddy calculations. But at some point, depending on currents and the state of the water, she would have to head for the mainland and abandon any plan of limping back to the island. Or not. But knowing which way to lean, knowing whether to risk it or not, was the million-dollar puzzle.

Meanwhile, she concentrated on rowing. It felt good to get some exercise, and the work warmed her. It had been cold the night before. The temperature had dropped off somewhere close to zero, she estimated. Everything had become brittle and sharp and no one moved from the fire if she or he could help it. But now, with the sun only a yellow mist at the edge of the sea, she liked digging the oars into the water and pulling backward. Some of her best memories revolved around rowing.

When she had brought the boat maybe two hundred yards off shore, she stopped to bail. The water seeped in steadily, for sure, but at least it hadn't frozen. It remained liquid, doubtless from the salt content, and she scooped, poured, scooped, poured for a full five minutes before setting forth again.

The island, when she checked it as she resumed rowing, had suddenly slipped sideways on her. *Tides*, she thought. *Or currents*. Apparently the currents were fairly stiff, because they had moved the boat a fair distance off course after only a short interval of bailing. That was interesting. She made a mental note to keep that in mind when she made her calculation about going forward or retreating.

The water, when she scanned the sea behind her, had smoothed into a piece of black ice. Even the gulls that rode the tiny swells hardly moved. Now and then she felt a braid of water tuck against the bow of the boat, a current, she imagined, wrapping around the island and carrying everything out to sea. With luck, she thought, someone on a boat would see her and swing by. Eventually boats had to pass by the island, she knew, but for the time being it was Thanksgiving weekend and people were busy. It struck her as uncanny when she thought about how many things had worked against them on this trip. It started with the quake. Who had ever heard of an earthquake in Maine hurting anyone? But it had caught them at just the wrong moment and everything had snowballed from there. Black Friday weekend, being in the magazine when the quake hit, the fact that there was a quake at all, the wall collapsing on the camp supplies, poor Azzy, poor Sam, the decision not to allow electronics on the trip, the fact that their emergency phone had been near the wall and had been covered along with the food . . .

It was astonishing, really, how poorly things had gone.

And it was astonishing, she realized now as she rowed deeper toward the center point of the crossing, how strong the currents had turned out to be. They were no joke. She performed a little experiment by lifting up her oars and focusing her eyes on a landmark – a Citgo tower marking a gas station, barely visible on the horizon line – and watched to see what the current would do to the boat. She tried to triangulate, estimating various points and distances, but the sea made it tricky. No question, though, that the currents pushed against her and tried to carry her out to sea.

Part of the problem was the boat was too darn heavy.

It dug into the current. Its heaviness, its waterlogged state, made it a more generous target for the currents. If it had been light and crisp, the tides might have affected it less. But the skiff moved like an old turtle, heavy and ponderous, and it was that sluggish quality that started to itch in Ursula's thinking.

I should turn around, she thought. *I should do it now.*

Water lapped around her feet. The boat settled more comfortably into the sea. She felt a little tug of dread begin to pull whenever she touched the oars. Things weren't going exactly as planned.

On the way back from the designated latrine area, Harry spotted a boat on the horizon. It was hard to say what it was, but it looked like a tanker. It stretched a long way on the edge of the world, its smoky discharge faintly visible in the calmness. He stopped to watch it for a moment. He dug his hand into his pocket and felt for the harmonica. He lifted it out and put it to his lips, tasting the woodsmoke from the fire the night before. He blew up and down the holes, then slapped the spit out against his jeans.

He started to put the harmonica back when he happened to see Ms. Carpenter sitting on the ocean.

At least it looked that way. She sat on the ocean.

He had to rub his eyes a little and tell himself to concentrate. The evidence of his eyes didn't make much sense. What was Ms. Carpenter doing out on the water in the first place? And where was the boat? He took a step forward, as if that tiny distance would help to explain everything. He squinted and held his hand up to shade his eyes from the emerging sun. In tiny heartbeats, the meaning of his vision became clear.

The boat was under her. And she was sinking.

"Hey," he yelled. "Hey."

But he doubted she heard him. She was a long ways off, drifting in the direction of the tanker, and now and then he saw water pour away from the boat. It was peculiar to see.

It took a second for it all to register. She was bailing. That was what happened when the water spilled out in an arc from the boat. The currents had carried her out to sea, and now the boat wallowed in the smooth surface of the water, and she was in all kinds of trouble.

"Hey," he yelled again, as if that might help some way.

Then he turned back to the fire and started to run as fast as he could.

Less than a minute later, Mr. Puffin and the others ran up behind him to see what had happened. He lifted his finger and pointed out to Ms. Carpenter in the boat. In the sinking boat.

"Look!" he said. "The boat!"

People skidded to a stop around him. They followed the line of his finger until their eyes picked Ms. Carpenter's dory from the background of the sea. The sun had moved higher in the sky now and Harry saw her more clearly. She did look to be sitting in the sea, but that was an optical illusion because the boat rode so heavily and close to the water.

"Oh, no," Mr. Puffin said. "What is she doing? What has she done?"

Then Harry felt everyone finally comprehend. He got it, too. She hadn't meant to go in that direction. Why would she? There was nothing that way, no hint of salvation farther out to sea. The currents had her. That was the only answer that made sense.

"What do we do?" Sandy Bellow asked. "Why is she out there?"

"The currents . . ." Mr. Puffin said and then looked away, his eyes tearing up.

"The boat is too heavy," Bob Worm said. "She should have waited."

"You mean she can't get back *here*?" Sandy asked, her voice rising into a cry on the last word.

"We don't know that yet," Mr. Puffin said.

But they did know it, Harry realized. They knew it as plain as day. Ms. Carpenter had made a horrible mis-calculation. That was a big *duh*, Harry knew.

"We can't help her," Mary said, her voice level with amazement. "We can't do anything for her."

"Maybe when she gets behind the island, the current won't be so bad," Harry said.

He said it just to say it. He didn't believe it.

He felt a shiver run up his spine. Ms. Carpenter wasn't going to make it back. That was the long and short of it. She had gone out to sea in a leaky boat and in no time the currents had taken her away. She couldn't swim for it. Not easily, and not with the water so cold. She wouldn't make it the length of a pool.

"We can use a human microphone," Mary said. "Do you guys know what that is?"

It took Harry a second to realize someone had spoken to them.

When no one answered, Mary explained.

"We start by saying *mic check*. Then whatever the speaker says, everyone repeats. You use short sentences. People use it for protests."

"Try it," Mr. Puffin said.

Mary said, "Mic check."

Everyone repeated it.

"Louder," she said.

"Louder," they repeated.

"I don't know what to say," Mary whispered.

"Mic check," Mr. Puffin said.

They said, "Mic check."

"Don't fight the current," he said.

"Don't fight the current," they repeated.

"Go with it," he said.

"Go with it," they yelled.

Then he stopped. The sound went out onto the sea and flung itself back at them. Harry watched the boat and saw Ms. Carpenter raise her hand for a moment, attempt to wave, or ask them to join her, and then the silence returned and the sound of the gulls became a regular riot of noise and insult.

She had to swim for it. That thought slowly lodged into Ursula Carpenter's mind. The thought came sideways, crabbing in, and she tried to resist it as long as possible. The sea was cold. The sea was *horribly* cold, a fact she had already confirmed by sitting shin deep in the water, the bailer no longer able to match the slow bubble of incoming water. It astonished her how quickly it had all fallen apart. She had merely rowed out a couple hundred yards, testing the water, when the currents had taken the boat like a willful hand and pushed it out to sea.

She heard them yelling, then silence. She raised her hand, waved, then returned to bailing as fast as she could. Each time she stopped rowing, the current carried her farther away from the island.

After the yelling – what had they meant by it? What were they trying to say? – she twisted around to see behind her. She wondered if the current might take her past another island. It was becoming clear to her that she could not fight the current current. She smiled at that little joke, a tight, bright smile that nearly pained her to shut down. *Current current.* That was pretty good, she thought. That was an okay joke given her circumstances.

She did not like to think about going into the sea. She had watched too many shark documentaries and though it was unlikely that any sharks patrolled the cold waters outside of Casco Bay, you could never say that for certain. There probably *were* sharks, at least bottom-feeding nurse sharks and the like, but what she feared most of all was a great white. A great white surging up from the bottom, that was her nightmare. She didn't want to leave the water and know that a shark had taken her into the air, that coming down into the white splash she would find the shark's dead black eye holding her gaze. So even if the water was cold and would probably do her in long before she had to worry about sharks, she still didn't like the thought.

She stopped bailing and pulled frantically on the oars for at least three minutes. The boat moved sluggishly. It moved like a sunken bathtub, and the harder she rowed, she judged, the more quickly the water came through the old cracks. Pushing the dry, flaking bow through the waves only made it leak faster, harder, fuller. That left absolutely no options available.

Except swimming, a little voice mentioned again in her brain. *Except swimming for shore.*

She was aware, too, that every minute delayed only made the potential swim longer. She was not getting closer to the island. In fact, the current moved her directly away. If she was going to swim, it was time to swim. Delay only made things worse.

She stopped to bail again. The paint can leaked whenever she submerged it and drew it out. The boat beneath her had changed in her imagination. She pictured it now as an old brown leaf, maybe from an oak, and it swirled and fell, drifted and sank like an oak leaf on a soft autumn afternoon. And what was she? She was an ant or a young caterpillar riding the leaf on its fall, drifting for a moment above the grassy meadow, falling near the old stone wall she had always loved near her house. Each fall she had gone outside and sat on a special rock, directly beneath a mother oak, and she had read poetry and let her attention be divided between the words on the page and the sweet-scented fall of the autumn leaves. Later she would go inside and drink hot chocolate, or perhaps her mother would have made her special kale and sausage soup, and all of it stayed mixed with the sense of falling leaves and the world spinning toward colder weather.

She had those thoughts in mind when the water finally pushed over the gunwale of the boat. She sat for a moment suspended – not sinking, not truly floating, either, but calm in a way she had never been calm before. The boat began to settle more fully beneath her. She tried the oars again, but she no longer cared if they worked or not. The boat made a short, quiet pop and then began going down, down, and she spread her arms on the water and felt the cold enter her bloodstream and she no longer felt a separation between the sea and her body.

PART FOUR

SEAWEED

SURVIVAL TIP #4

Both cold and hot weather are a threat if you have no food. But extreme heat and cold will kill you in other ways before you have a chance at starvation. In terms of living without food, heat means faster dehydration — cold means more energy is burned to keep the body's temperature at a cozy 98.6 degrees Fahrenheit (37 degrees Celsius). If you're lucky enough to be in mild temperatures, you'll be able to live a little longer without food.

CHAPTER 11

Mary carried an armful of seaweed back to the fire. It smelled horrible and made her arms damp and cold, but it was the best she could do. They had eaten three armfuls already, each one spread around the fire on big rocks to help it dry. When it gained enough heat from the rocks and the fire, they ate it like fried onions. It tasted of salt and the sea, but at least, Mary thought, it gave her stomach something to do. She wondered, though, if it only made her hungrier in the long run.

They had been more determined about finding food after Ms. Carpenter had disappeared. Her disappearance had made them all more resolute. Even Sandy Bellow, Mary saw, carried seaweed up from the shoreline, where the team collected it. She held it out and away from her, squeamish about getting water on her clothes, but at least she carried it.

Things could happen. That was the lesson Ms. Carpenter's disappearance had taught them all.

Mary unloaded her armful of seaweed carefully. She felt shaky and cold. When she finished she went to see how Sam was faring. Sam had been Ms. Carpenter's special charge, but now that had been turned upside down. She went to the tent and zipped the zipper down. Then she stuck her head in, trying to see Sam in the dimness. He didn't move.

"Sam, are you awake?" she whispered, testing his sleep.

To her astonishment, his eyes opened immediately.

"I'm hungry," he whispered.

"We don't have anything except seaweed. Sorry."

"That's okay," he said, but whether that meant it was okay, he wanted some, or okay, let it pass, she couldn't tell.

He didn't say anything else for a little while. It felt warm inside the tent. It also smelled funky, like a boys' locker room or the inside of the cafeteria on tuna day.

"I want to get out of the tent," he said. "If you'll help me."

"Do you need to go to the bathroom? I can call one of the guys."

"No, I just want to get out of the tent. It's making me a little crazy."

She helped him. It took him a long time to get his shoes on and to work his way slowly onto his feet, but he stood finally. She stayed close to him and let him lean on her when he needed it. When Bob Worm and Harry came back carrying seaweed, they both whistled and fist-bumped Sam. He obliged them, but it was clear it exhausted him to perform the slightest function. Mary propped him up on the best rock near the fire.

"This feels good," he said. "It's good to be out of the tent."

"I can't believe you're up and walking. Wait until Mr. Puffin sees you," Harry said, his hands busy stretching the seaweed out on the rocks surrounding the fire.

"They thought you were way down for the count," Bob Worm said.

"I don't remember much," Sam said. "Not after the first shake."

"You got it bad," Bob said. "Whammo. You looked horrible."

"What day is it, anyway?" he asked.

"It's Monday, around noon," Mary said. "The lobster boat guy should be here in about twenty-four hours. We're going to make it."

Mr. Puffin came back then. Mary watched him take in the fact that Sam had emerged from the tent, not looking great, obviously, but at least not dying. Mary saw the calculation enter Mr. Puffin's expressions: his colleague, Ms. Carpenter, had given her life to bring help earlier for Sam. Now Sam was here, and Ms. Carpenter wasn't.

"Glad to see you up, Sam," Mr. Puffin said carefully.

"I just needed to get out of the tent."

Mr. Puffin nodded. Sandy came back again, this time carrying barely a handful of seaweed. No one pointed it out. No one had the energy to point out every shortcut Sandy employed.

"We're all here," Mr. Puffin said, taking a position beside the fire. "We're all going to make it. If we work together, we'll be okay."

"We're running low on wood," Bob Worm pointed out.

"Well, we'll cut back a little on it. Everyone hear that? Be smart about the wood. Don't add more than we need at any one point."

Then a loud cawing sound drowned everything else out. Bob Worm and Harry shouted and turned and ran off, yelling for everyone to come. When nobody did, Harry turned back and shouted to them all, the veins on either side of his neck tight strings.

"We caught a seagull! We trapped him! Come on, dinner is served!"

Mostly, it had been Harry's doing. That's what Bob Worm thought when he ran up to the old lobster pot and saw the gull beating its wings against the wire sides. The door – Harry had figured out a drop mechanism, so that any vibration brought the door down and trapped whatever was inside – had worked beautifully. It bounced occasionally when the gull rammed it, but two rocks secured it and Bob knew it wouldn't release. No, they had fresh meat for dinner.

"I can't believe it worked!" Harry yelled, hopping and jumping over the rocks that lined the shore. He looked like a leprechaun, Bob thought, clicking his heels and leaping around after a pot of gold. But this was better than gold. If they could catch one seagull, they could catch more, presumably. That put an *X* through the hunger problem. They could find water and feed themselves, albeit in a pretty bleak fashion. Still, survival was survival, and Bob Worm slapped Harry's back when they finally arrived over the pot.

"What do you say?" Bob said, feeling good for the first time since they had left the lobster boat. "Pretty cool, huh?"

"I can't believe the bait worked. It was lousy bait."

It had been a jellyfish, three small dead minnows, and a worm-type thing that grossed Harry out just to touch it. But it had worked. The gull had stepped inside, and its movement had sprung the door. Bob wasn't surprised to see that the gull had eaten the three minnows right away. That's how much calories mean, he thought. That was the importance of every bite and every meal.

Mr. Puffin came up beside him.

"It's a herring gull," he said. "You can eat him."

"Are there kinds you can't eat?" asked Harry.

Mr. Puffin shrugged. He squatted down to examine the lobster cage. He flicked the door a little and watched it close sharply on its makeshift hinges.

"I'm impressed," he said, standing again.

"You're not just going to kill it, are you?" Sandy asked.

"No, *you* are," Bob said, just to be a smart aleck.

"Are you going to eat it raw?" Sandy asked. "We don't have a way to cook it."

"We can put it on skewers and roast it," Bob said. "You don't have to eat it if you don't want."

"Save the guts for bait," Harry said.

But the matter of killing the bird still remained, Bob knew. No one stepped forward. It was one thing to catch a bird, as miraculous as that was, but it was another to wring its neck. Bob knew enough about raising chickens to understand there wouldn't be much meat on the seagull. Maybe ten good bites, he estimated, then a bunch of slurping and cracking. They could eat the guts, too, he realized. People ate the gizzard when they ate turkeys, plus the lungs and heart and liver. The truly gross parts he would use for bait.

Bob had almost persuaded himself to step forward and dig his hands into the trap, when a tiny tremor moved across the island. It made everything shake, though it was nowhere as large or as forceful as the earlier tremors had been. It felt like an after-aftershock, something that marked the end of the blip that had caused the shaking in the first place. Still, it made everyone look around in mild discomfort.

"What's going on?" Sandy asked with her nasal voice obnoxiously raised. "Why does this keep happening?"

"We're okay," Mr. Puffin said.

"It doesn't *feel* okay," Sandy said. "It feels horrible."

Then the tremor disappeared and the birds, the gulls, raised their voices and screamed. Bob Worm stepped forward and opened the gate on the lobster pot. He held it open while the bird, panicked at first, then slowly gaining confidence, slipped past him and flapped away. No one said anything. Bob looked at Harry, who merely shrugged and turned to go back to the fire.

"Why did you do that?" Mary asked. "I thought we were going to eat it."

Bob shrugged. He didn't know why he let it go, but no one said anything else about it. It was just too much, he thought. The whole thing was just too much.

"Hey," Sam Harding called, "who wants a piece of a Snickers bar?"

Silence. Then someone, it sounded like Bob Worm, said, "Saaaayyy whaaaaatttt?"

Sam heard them wrestle their way to the tent, all of them laughing. Someone zipped the zipper down and stuck a hand through. Sam gave them the Snickers. Mary said over and over, "No way! No way!"

"Divide it up evenly," Harry yelled. "No cheating."

"I can't believe we have a Snickers bar," Sandy said. "*Three* Snickers bars! Where were they?"

"Inside my sneakers. A spare pair. I just didn't look before."

Sam wanted to get out and join them, but he felt tired suddenly. He felt tired and his head refused to stop ringing. It was a high, plaintive bell sound that filled the inside of his head and he hated it but couldn't chase it away.

"Snickers bars!" Harry yelled in a happy, surprised voice, apparently calling to Mr. Puffin. "Real Snickers bars."

Sam tried to hear Mr. Puffin's reaction, but he drifted off again before he could catch all of the conversation. When he woke again, he heard them discussing the temperature. It was getting colder. He felt it even inside the tent. He felt it in his back, radiating up from the ground. He tried to remember what his bed felt like, what it felt like to take a shower and to be warm, but those things seemed from another life.

Then he heard someone suggest they move back into the magazine. Just for the night. Just to be out of the wind and to be a little warmer. He tried to stay with the conversation, but sleep tugged him away again. For a moment he imagined himself deep under his covers in his own bed, freshly showered, homework finished, everything safe and warm and clean. The seagulls made a sound like someone screaming, *yes, yes, yes,* and that sound sent him deeper into sleep.

CHAPTER 12

The wind made a sound like a woman keening for her man lost at sea. It kept pulling thick, unhappy sounds from the slot in the magazine wall. They had already tried a fire, but the fire pushed out too much smoke and there was nowhere for it to go. Bob Worm had talked about pushing a hole through the roof, but that had been voted down as too dangerous. As a result, they sat in near darkness, like cave people, Mary thought, and shivered and tried anything to stay warm.

"He comes tomorrow, though," Sandy said for the umpteenth time.

Meaning the lobsterman comes tomorrow, Mary reflected. Meaning they would be rescued tomorrow.

"At noon," Mr. Puffin said because someone had to say something each time Sandy said it.

"I'm going to have the world's biggest soda," Sandy said. "I have an enormous craving for it. I don't know why."

"I want a steak," Bob Worm said. "A juicy one with a side of potatoes."

"Tomorrow," Sandy said, her voice wrapping it in prayer tones.

"Let's get through what we need to get through," Mr. Puffin said. "Then we can think about everything else."

"I'm starving now," Harry said. "I didn't know I could get this hungry and not die. The candy bar only made it worse."

"It *was* better before the candy bar," Bob Worm agreed.

Sandy did not think her share of the Snickers bars had been a fair portion. Three bars divided among six people was not rocket science. But they didn't have a knife or a ruler, so they had broken her bar apart in what was supposed to be an equitable way, but it clearly didn't work.

Half a bar was half a bar. Sandy's piece, she was absolutely certain, was smaller than the piece they gave to Mary.

She almost didn't care. She was sick of the whole situation. She didn't dare say anything about the Snickers bar, because of course everyone would see her as being a *complainicus*. That's what her mother always said when Sandy voiced an objection.

"Quit being such a complainicus," she would say. "Who are you, a Roman general named Complainicus?"

But half a Snickers bar was half a Snickers bar, and anyone who knew anything could certainly agree with that.

"We could be eating a nice seagull right now," Harry said. "If we hadn't all chickened out."

Then Mary hissed for everyone to be quiet.

She heard an engine. At least she *thought* she heard an engine. It was hard to tell. The interior of the magazine echoed and the voices, everyone's voices, blocked the sounds from outdoors. She hissed again and held out her hand, patting it down in a signal to be quiet, and everyone looked at her strangely. But she held up a finger, pointed to her ear, and then made them all listen.

It was an engine. A boat engine.

Mary went through the doorway first. She was the most nimble, she knew, and she didn't wait to see who came second. She stopped for an instant to locate the sound – *from the water, duh*, she told herself – and then darted off to the east end where they had originally landed.

The ground was not easy going. About four inches of icy rain had fallen and turned everything slick and greasy. She skidded around the first corner of the fort, nearly fell, then managed to jerk her body back upright. As she slid down the bank toward the sea, she spotted the boat slipping past the island, its lights bright and happy and purposeful.

"Hey . . . help, help us!" she screamed.

Behind her an entire chorus joined in.

"Help," they yelled. "Hey. Help, hey . . ."

They had forgotten about *mic check*, Mary realized too late.

The boat did not pause. It was hard to see exactly what it was, what kind of vessel, but it looked like a lobster boat, a blue one, a different color than Bertie's. It looked like someone returning to port, Mary thought, after checking his pots.

"Did they hear us?" Sandy asked. "Did they hear?"

No one answered. But the wind rose up and kicked them in the tail, and Mary turned around and headed back to the magazine.

Now the cold was the issue, Eamon thought.

The issue changed faster than he could keep track of it. First it had been the rocks falling from the tremors, then it had been water, then it had been food, then it had been Sam's worsening health, then it had been Ursula, then it had been the wind, then it had been the boat slipping past and condemning them to more time on the island . . .

And now it was the cold. The fierce, relentless cold.

They needed a fire, and they needed to be out of the wind and storm, and those things didn't work together. Not a bit.

This time of year, he calculated, sunrise came later. Call it seven fifteen or so before the sun would appear. Until then they had to rest inside their lair like animals. He guessed it was somewhere around four. He wanted to ask Bob, but Bob was asleep.

For a time he dozed. When he woke, his mind went to the newest issue.

Wood.

Fuel. They were running out. If Bertie showed up promptly at noon, they would be okay. But if anything interfered with the pickup, if weather made it difficult for Bertie to retrieve them, then the cold would become serious indeed. They could not endure too many days of such sharp temperatures. Not on top of food deprivation and exposure.

He sat up. He didn't want those thoughts racing around in his head.

"I'm freezing," Sandy said from her position on the ground not far from him. "Is anyone else freezing?"

"I'm pretty cold," Harry said.

"We should take turns in the tent," Mary said. "Two by two. We brought it inside for Sam, but we all need to use it. We can lie close together. Give everyone a half hour at a time and see if we can warm up."

"What about Sam?" Bob Worm asked.

"Sam's going to have to share some of his heat," Mary answered.

It was true, Eamon thought. It was the best plan given the circumstances.

He watched — as much as he could in the dimness — Mary crawl across the space and zip down the tent flap. She said something to Sam and then Sam slowly came out of the tent.

"Sandy, come on," Mary said. "Someone time us. We get fifteen minutes, maybe. We'll keep this bag warm."

"We're going to squeeze in together?" Sandy asked.

"That's the plan unless you have a better one."

Eamon heard them making their way into the single sleeping bag. He worried about Sam. It must be frightfully cold, he thought, to come out of a warm sleeping bag and find yourself in a rocky dungeon.

"You okay, Sam?" Eamon asked the boy.

Sam said yes, but Eamon could hear the cold covering him.

"You know, I was thinking," Sam said after a little while. "We should make teams. We should never have a boat go by like that and not have someone outside to signal."

"You're right," Eamon said and he knew it was true. "Maybe we've been a little lazy because Bertic should be back soon. But we should prepare for the worst and be happy when things turn out better."

"We could divide into fuel, water, signal," Bob Worm said.

Yes, Eamon thought. Why hadn't he thought of that before?

"We'll start at sunrise. Fuel is food, too, so that team has to bring seaweed. We should have three teams working all the time. It's stupid that we haven't."

"We keep thinking Bertie will solve things," Bob Worm said. "If we knew we had to be here for a month, we'd have a different attitude."

"Still, it's a good idea to break out in teams," Eamon said. "It will give us some structure. We need structure."

"Or we'll turn savage," Bob Worm said.

For reasons Eamon couldn't quite name, everyone laughed. He didn't know, but he laughed as hard as anyone. It felt a little like going crazy, but it felt good, too. Then Harry pulled out his harmonica and played an old cowboy song. This time, though, the songs didn't make you sad. They made you feel like maybe you had a chance after all. At sunrise, Eamon promised himself, they would set up a new camp and get serious about making work teams.

CHAPTER 13

Bertie was nowhere to be seen. It was noon on Tuesday, Sandy knew, and Bertie was nowhere on the horizon. It frosted her to think about it. Where was he? What was he doing? How could he be late to pick them up off the island? She didn't care what kind of explanation he tried to give later on, she wouldn't buy it. Not for an instant. On time was on time, and lateness was a choice. That was what her grandfather had always said and she had never fully understood it until this moment.

Whatever her grandfather said or didn't say hardly mattered now. The only thing that mattered was the sight of Bertie pulling up in his little lobster boat.

"Where is he?" she asked aloud.

She knew it was a mistake to ask. People didn't like other people who asked hard questions. People didn't like *her* when she asked them.

"Sandy, if I knew, I'd tell you," Mr. Puffin said.

"Jeez, Sandy, give it a rest," Bob Worm said. "You're not making it any better by asking every ten seconds."

"Noon, right? He said noon."

What good was it to argue with them? She was deathly sick of them all. If they knew so much about everything, how come this disaster had befallen them in the first place? She would like to have asked them that little riddle. But they needed her to be the nag and scold, the person who asked all the questions and then ate all the responses. She had lived that role her entire life. It was nothing new.

"What's our plan if he doesn't show up?" Sandy asked. "Do we just sit here?"

"We don't have a plan," Mr. Puffin said. "I'm open to suggestions, though."

"We should start collecting wood and seaweed while there's light to work with," Mary said. "Break back into our teams just in case."

"I have to think he would be early if anything," Harry said. "Don't fishermen wake up early? Isn't that their deal?"

Sandy stood and moved her position to get more squarely into the sun. They sat on a half-dozen boulders near the landing area. The sun felt good. It wasn't warm, exactly, but at least it was direct and threw their shadows around them. That counted for something. The stones underneath them held what little heat the sun produced. It felt good to sit on them, especially when the wind stopped for a second.

"I suppose we might as well work while we're waiting," Mr. Puffin said. "Let's break into two teams, one for wood, one for food."

"What kind of guy did you hire, anyway? Is it so hard to be on time?" Sandy asked.

"He's a local fisherman, Sandy," Mr. Puffin said, his voice tight and controlled, "who knows these waters and knows this island. He has a dependable boat. I don't know why he's not here now, but he said it would be *around* noon. Around noon. Is that clear?"

"He should be here," Sandy said.

Mr. Puffin stood and walked away, heading toward the waterline, where they often found driftwood. She didn't care if he was annoyed with her. She was annoyed with him, so let that go down on the record books as a tie, she reflected. Just because he was the teacher didn't make him an expert about everything. She just wanted to go home, take a shower, and forget any of this ever happened.

One by one the others followed Mr. Puffin. Everyone except Sam, who had found two rocks together in the sunlight and had stretched out on them, dozing. It was hard to figure Sam, Sandy thought. Sometimes he seemed to be faking his illness, then other times he seemed like he was going to croak any second. She couldn't read him.

"My parents will bring legal action," Sandy said, baiting Sam with that little morsel. "Don't think they won't. Mr. Puffin may be all high and mighty out here, but wait till he has to go back and face the music. Face the legal proceedings that will come from this lame adventure on Puffin Island."

"It's not Puffin Island, you dope," Sam said, his arm tucked over his eyes to keep the sun out.

"I'm just saying. We *all* have legal cases to bring."

"You're alive, aren't you? What could you sue about?"

"How about mental anguish?" Sandy said, her voice surprising her with its anger. "About the cruelty of keeping us here without supplies."

"The rocks fell on the supplies."

"Not my problem."

"Well, what was Mr. Puffin supposed to do about that? The supplies are buried."

"Oh, gee, let me see. Well, he insisted we not bring cell phones, didn't he? Think one of those might be handy about now?"

"He was doing a thing," Sam said. "A trip thing. You know what he was doing."

She stood up on one of the rocks and looked toward the mainland. Nothing. Nothing at all.

In the late-afternoon light, Eamon studied the rock slide below the fort wall for a long time. It wasn't the first time he had looked at it, but now, with Bertie not appearing, the situation had become more desperate. Specifically, he wondered if he could creep around and probe into some of the hollows to check for food. It didn't look entirely unsafe, but he didn't trust his judgment. His judgment had led them to the island in the first place, and had put them in the magazine exactly when the quake had hit, and it had contributed to Ursula's disappearance in the boat.

When he stood back and assessed the rocks objectively, the area resembled a mousetrap. The scattered blocks of granite spread out on the ground replicated the wooden base of the mousetrap. The backpacks and tents served as the cheese. And the spring-loaded metal hasp that snapped down? The teetering rock wall provided that little hazard. The wall stood stiffly enough in the sharp wind that broke from the landward side of the island, but if a tremor came, or if anything happened to give way, then whoever was underneath it was going to be pulp.

Hunger on one side of the balance. The mousetrap on the other.

Someone would have to come for them soon, he thought. It was pointless to risk any more lives. As long as they had water, they would survive. Long before anyone starved to death, they would be rescued. That simply stood to reason. So it made no sense whatsoever to creep around on the fallen rocks, sticking your hands and arms into the hollow places. No sense to be an ant on a pile of spilled sugar cubes.

And even though he knew better, he began walking toward it.

"I give you permission to eat me," Bob Worm said. "I mean if things go bad, really bad. Have at it. I won't mind."

Harry laughed. Everyone laughed. Bob Worm, to Harry's amazement, had turned out to be pretty funny. Bob Worm had an armful of wood – scraps, really, and twigs from shrubs that wouldn't burn at all, Harry knew – and he led the procession back to the campsite. The sun had already begun to slide into the forest over on the mainland. Bertie wasn't coming, Harry knew. Something had happened to Bertie. They had all worked through the calendar carefully as they collected wood, matching events with days, and they had agreed one and all that today was Tuesday and they were scheduled to be met by Bertie.

On the other side of the situation, things were not good. Harry knew that. They were heading back to camp and they only had a little wood. They could do the two-in-the-sleeping-bag routine again, but if the temperature dropped further still even that wouldn't save them. Clear nights bring low temperatures, Harry knew.

They needed a fire and they needed to be inside, but they couldn't stay inside with the fire because the smoke drove them out. Harry had an idea he wanted to try. He had seen a pile of old cans and metal up on the ridge to the seaward side of the island, and he wondered about a brown metal drum he had spotted. He wondered if they couldn't fashion it into a stove. A stove was the thing. If they could set up a stove in the magazine, then they would have the best of both worlds: heat and shelter. With a little luck, a stove could heat up the stonework in the magazine. They might actually be comfortable for a few hours.

When they got back to the campsite, Harry grabbed Bob Worm and explained his idea.

"It's worth a try," Bob Worm said. "Let's go."

It only took a few minutes to find the metal pile. It went deeper than Harry had anticipated. It represented years and years of junk – tin cans, cleaning bottles, anything you could imagine around a house. The tin drum Harry had spotted earlier was in rough shape, but it was still in one piece. He tried to see what had been stored inside the drum. It looked like oil or kerosene or something that smelled of petroleum. With Bob's help, he turned the barrel upside down and let it drain. Then he looked around for piping and found a length of something that looked like a rusted exhaust pipe for a muffler.

"We can try that," he told Bob Worm. "We can use that to vent the stove."

"Through the slot?" Bob asked.

Harry nodded.

"Not bad," Bob Worm said. "Where did you learn how to do this stuff? The seagull trap and everything?"

"My dad is a wannabe inventor. He's always down in the basement messing around. I guess I picked it up."

"Let's try it."

But it was not easy. Not only did it take them a long time to get the barrel down to the mouth of the magazine, it also took a superhuman effort to squeeze it through the opening Mary had pioneered. It made a lot of noise and it rolled when you didn't want it to roll, and as they worked with it Harry realized they needed vents. They had to draw air in, then let it escape. That was the basic airflow with a stove. With decent tools, it might have been a reasonably easy job, but the only way to punch holes into the barrel was to use sharp stones. Eventually, though, they had the barrel up on two rocks for support and they had hooked the exhaust pipe to a punched hole in the center of the body. They hammered away a portion of the front of the stove so they could shove wood into the fire.

"Ready to try it?" Harry asked when they had it where they wanted it.

Bob nodded. Everyone had gathered around. Even if the stove failed, at least it gave them something to root for, Harry reflected. That was worth something on the face of it.

Bob made a small fire, using some of the charcoal from the outside fire as a bed. The dried pine went up immediately, giving a wonderful light. Carefully, Harry and Bob fed twigs to the fire. Smoke escaped – you couldn't pretend that it didn't – but the main share of it went up the exhaust pipe. It was tolerable, Harry thought. It was possible to stay next to the stove as long as you didn't stand and get a face full of the smoke that collected near the ceiling.

"Well, look at that," Bob said. "Pretty slick, isn't it?"

"It's warm," Mary said. "It's actually getting warm."

"I hope it doesn't explode," Harry said. "It's anyone's guess what was inside it."

But he felt good. He felt proud. The stove was the best idea anyone had had in a while. It conserved wood and gave greater heat than an open fire. The room of the magazine, if they had sufficient wood, might actually get warm. That was something of a miracle. Harry bent close to the stove and held out his hands. Heat radiated off the sides of the barrel.

"Not sure how hot we can get it," Bob Worm said. "Might be too rusty. It could burn up itself."

"Just keep it small, then," Mary said. "Just nice and easy."

Harry fed the sticks to Bob, who in turn fed the sticks to the fire. The fire burned at a calm, steady rate. Coals eventually formed at the bottom.

They were still working to establish the fire when Sam came through the opening of the magazine.

"Hey, you guys," he said, his voice excited, "there are five seals down by the boat landing. I saw them come ashore. They're right down there."

An ant on a pile of sugar cubes, Eamon thought.

That was probably a mixed metaphor. Before he had imagined the rock slide as a mousetrap, but now he had the ant image going through his brain. It had something to do with the slowness he had to employ to get anywhere. The rocks were incredibly slick, glazed as they were with ice and salt and who knew what else. Most of the time he had to travel in a kind of apelike four-point crawl, moving slowly from point to point. *Another meta-phor*, he reminded himself. *Mice and apes and ants.*

He did not look at the rock wall dangling above him. If he permitted himself to look at the wall, he realized, he would not be able to move. At least he knew now that he had made the correct decision to forbid any of the students to crawl around in search of food. It was a stupid, dangerous thing to do. He knew it was stupid, and he knew it was dangerous, but he did it anyway . . .

. . . because some way or another he had to pay for his first stupid decision to bring them here.

That was the truth. Terrible as it was, that was why he kept crawling across the rocks, risking his life for the possibility of finding a backpack. It was not rational and it was not intelligent, but it felt like paying for his mistake.

Let the rocks fall if they had to, he reflected. He would rather perish trying to do something good at last than sit like an idiot and let more harm come to his student group.

He was thinking that way when a rock fell from the wall.

It was not a big rock, and he did not hear it leave the wall, but suddenly it exploded near him with a violence that shocked him. It *sparked*! It sparked against the bottom rocks when it landed. Then a piece of the rock flew off and splintered in a somersault, and he crabbed to one side away from it, hoping that if more rocks came he would be out of harm's way. Adrenaline slipped into his bloodstream and made him breathe through his mouth. His fingers skidded off a handhold and he slammed down, jamming his cheek against a slab of granite. He felt his teeth crack against the rock and he let out a sharp, painful breath of air, and he caught himself with his shoulder, jamming it down, and when he stopped moving he saw a bright-green tent directly below him.

There. Right there, his mind whispered. *You've got it now.*

He had blood in his mouth and his teeth felt wobbly and smashed on one side, but he had found a tent. A green, lovely tent. Slowly, slowly, he lowered his hand down into the hole and his finger grazed the nylon of the tent. It was smashed and pounded down, but he could distinguish lumps inside it. He knew the lumps had to be a backpack, maybe one with food, and so he lowered himself more, pressing into the stones, reaching in as someone reaches through a half-closed window for a jar of jam.

Please, please, please, he thought. *Please let me do this at least.*

He wished he had a longer arm. He wished the rocks were not so sharp and slimy.

At last his fingers grabbed the lump through the nylon. It was a backpack; he was nearly certain of it. He jammed his arm in farther, and he felt the tendons in his shoulder stretching too far. But he didn't care. He yanked and the backpack came up, but it was still wrapped inside the shell of the tent. He kept pulling anyway, and when the backpack was not too far beneath him, he propped it against a different rock and made sure it could no longer sink. As quickly as he could, he reached back and dug his penknife out of his pocket and he sliced around the base of the backpack. Part by part, the backpack came free, and as it did he heard another rock explode near him. Another fell, too, and this one sent a chip his way and he flinched and nearly dropped the backpack down the newly created hole. Instead he stuck the shoulder strap in his mouth and bit down on it, then he lifted and fell backward, and the backpack came out and nearly landed on top of him.

His mouth felt bloody, but he had retrieved a backpack at least. He sat for a moment panting, and so involved was he with his own drama that he nearly missed the kids hurrying past the rock pile on their way to the landing site.

Mary crept behind the rocks and tried to keep quiet. She hadn't seen the seals yet, but she heard them. They made sharp, empty barking sounds that sometimes came to them, and sometimes only swept out to sea.

Harry carried a makeshift spear. He had talked about hunting them.

Which was not realistic, Mary thought. Even if they managed to kill a seal – and she gave Harry credit, he was surprisingly talented with small machines and mechanical solutions to problems – what would they possibly do with all the blubber?

She doubted, too, that Mr. Puffin would permit it. Not that he had every say in the world at this point. But he was still a teacher, still technically in command, and she doubted he would approve an assault on a creature weighing several hundred pounds. Not now. Not this close to the finish line.

"Down there," Harry whispered close to her ear. "I can see one. They're big!"

"You think you can get him?" Bob Worm asked.

Harry shook his head. That was a sensible response, Mary thought.

Still, they continued to stalk the creatures. The seals were astonishing animals. Mary watched them bob their heads this way and that, taking rest but being talkative, too. It was not yet full evening and so they still had a bit of light by which to hunt. If they needed light. Mary realized she didn't know a thing about seals in any real sense.

"What kind are they?" someone whispered.

"Harbor seals," someone said.

"They smell like fish," Bob Worm said.

"I'm going to charge them," Harry said. "Just for fun."

"Don't," Mary said. "Let them be."

"I won't hurt them."

"They might hurt *you*," Bob Worm said. "They've got sharp teeth."

That stopped Harry, Mary saw. Sandy whispered that she was going back and that she was cold. Harry, though, couldn't resist entirely. He stood up suddenly and yelled a nonsense word, something like *cowabunga*, and the seal closest to the water slid in like a torpedo. Then a second one followed, but the third, a big, brutish-looking fellow, turned back and postured for a moment. Then he took to the water, too, while two others, out of eyesight, apparently jumped in also. Five sleek heads appeared in the water, all of them looking back. They looked human, Mary realized. Or like Labrador retrievers from the neck up.

And she was still staring at them, smiling hard and feeling good for the first time in days, when it suddenly occurred to her that the seals had been joined by a bright-blue sea kayak. And that kayak had been joined by another ten. The line of kayaks had been following the seals around the harbor, and they had come to the island as their last stop before calling it a night, and now Mary had somehow to piece the two visions together.

Seals and kayaks. Kayaks and seals.

"Hello," someone called from the boat, "did you have to scare them?"

Mary couldn't speak. She opened her mouth twice but nothing came out. Then she saw Mr. Puffin walking near them. He had a backpack in his hand and the side of his face looked swollen. He had blood on his shirt.

"Help!" Mr. Puffin called, his voice somehow broken and shaky. "We need help."

Mary had never heard anyone actually call for help before. She looked at Mr. Puffin and he said it again, this time swallowing it back so it broke in his chest and went nowhere.

CHAPTER 14

The leader's name was Ernest. He wore a rubberized wet suit and a yellow helmet, and a bright silver whistle dangled on his chest. Sam took in the details. The other kayakers ranged behind him, all of them whispering and repeating things down the line whenever Mr. Puffin explained something. You could tell Ernest was good at this kayaking stuff, because it was no joke to be out in these currents in near-winter conditions. But it was also a kind of challenge, and Ernest said several times they had been following seal groups and burning off their Thanksgiving dinner, no worries, and they had planned to be headed into port when they had stopped temporarily at the island to watch the seals up on shore.

"Then you scared them off," Ernest said, which he knew, which they *all* knew, was hardly the point at the moment.

"We don't know where Bertie is," Mr. Puffin said. "We expected to be picked up today."

"And the earthquake . . ." Ernest said, motioning with his chin toward the rock pile.

"Took everything."

"Well, we can help you with some food, and then we'll make a beeline to the mainland and get you a boat. We don't have a phone. Lucky we came by."

"It's very lucky," Sandy said.

"It's not even a mile to the mainland. We can make it in short order. You should be on a boat by sunset or a little later."

Meanwhile, Sam saw, one of the women in a rubber suit had gone from kayak to kayak, collecting food. She had parts of sandwiches and clementines and even a few packs of sweet-and-sour chips. Someone had a bunch of cookies in a Tupperware container, too, and they loaded the woman up as she went along.

"Here," she said, handing the food to Sandy. "I'm so sorry this happened to you."

It was everything Sam could do to stop from telling the woman that Sandy was the worst person to distribute the food. But before he could say anything, the woman looked at his ear. She didn't make a big fuss about it. She turned his head back and forth so she could see it better.

"You need to be cleaned up," she said. "This ear needs stitches."

"Are you a doctor?" Sam asked.

The woman nodded.

The kayakers reassembled in their boats a few yards out to sea. *It looks so easy*, Sam thought. It was easy for them, he reflected. It was just an afternoon's mini-adventure, a way to get outdoors on a late-fall weekend, and they had no idea that a drama had unfolded on the island. Seeing the boats paddle off, their strokes strong and rhythmic, made Sam wonder how he could capture such a thing on film. Maybe you couldn't. Maybe it was too strange for duplication.

"Pass the food around," Bob Worm said. "Let's divvy it up."

Then Sam noticed something. The others noticed it, too. Mr. Puffin had walked off a little distance and he had broken down. He had started crying, his shoulders rocking up and down, his grief, his anxiety, broken open and left for anyone to see.

Bob Worm ate four cookies, but the thing that surprised him most was the taste of the clementine. It was remarkable. He had only received half a fruit, maybe six tiny sections, but the flavor from the citrus was beyond description. He ate each section carefully, letting it slip and explode softly onto his tongue. He decided that he would eat a clementine every day of his life from this point forward. It was hands down the best thing he had ever eaten.

They sat around the last little bit of fire. No one had had the willpower to go back into the magazine. It didn't matter how cold it was. They burned everything they could find and didn't conserve anything.

Finally Harry said softly, "Here it comes."

Bob Worm looked toward the mainland and he saw the boat coming toward them. Rather, he saw the wake spreading out and spinning white against the gray-green ocean. A blue light turned on top of the boat, so Bob guessed it was probably Coast Guard. It came at a good clip.

"Whooo hoooooo," Sandy yelled, standing and wiggling her hips.

"Shut up, Sandy," Mary said.

But Sandy kept dancing. Bob couldn't say if he blamed her or not.

He felt a weird combination of emotions. Seeing Mr. Puffin crying had gotten them all twisted. It should have been fun and lighthearted – they were being rescued, after all – but it didn't feel that way. It felt clunky and strange, and though he didn't blame Sandy for celebrating, he also knew he couldn't join her. No way. He felt too upside down for that. He kept thinking of Azzy and Ms. Carpenter. Somehow while they were marooned on the island, the two deaths didn't seem quite real. They were part of this absurd adventure, and though he felt grief and sadness at their fates, he also felt he had to put it aside in order to survive.

But not anymore.

Now the full weight of what had happened hit him. It hit everyone, he guessed. They had created a sort of island morality, or island attitude, that now seemed hollow and strange. Bob couldn't get his thoughts straight. He only knew that people were coming who would ask a lot of questions. Who would spend time digging up rocks and searching the currents for an old leaky boat.

"Guess we should get ready," Mr. Puffin said. "Grab whatever you like."

But Bob knew, everyone knew, there was nothing to grab. When the time came, they pushed dirt over the fire and walked empty-handed toward the boat.

Harry left the island last. He hadn't meant to, then he did mean to. He had milled around the back of the group, letting people help them onto the boat. The guys who had come to rescue them were some kind of Delta Force, for goodness' sake. They hit the ground with blankets and hot soup, speaking with sharp commands, taking everything over. Way over. Harry was surprised to find himself resenting their treatment. It was good treatment, no mistake, but it was clinical and exact and it bothered the heck out of Harry. It felt like he was inside a drill.

Easy, easy, easy, he wanted to tell them.

He wasn't sure what he would have preferred, but it had something to do with pace. He wanted to mark the transition from the island to the boat, not merely let himself be swept away. He saw the same concern on Mr. Puffin's face. They had hit him hard with questions, firing one after another, and Mr. Puffin, shocked, had hardly been able to respond. Naturally the rescue team wanted answers, but the answers were not simple, and Mr. Puffin did not give a good account of himself in trying to answer them.

Leave him alone, Harry wanted to say. But he didn't.

So finally some muscle-headed guy with a broom mustache held out his hand and offered to pass him on board. As easy as that. Harry smiled. Then he turned back to the island and he wanted to make some sort of significant gesture, to say something memorable, but nothing came to mind. In the last glimmer of sunlight, pale and soft, he saw the tongue of stones sticking out toward him. Then he felt tears and a wild, crazy beating in his heart, and he ran up to where he had left the seal spear and he chucked it as hard as he could at the tongue of stones. It landed like a cheap stick, clanking a little, and one of the rescue guys clicked his tongue.

"Okay?" the guy asked when Harry returned to the boat.

"Okay," Harry said and he climbed on the boat.

Dead engine. Dead of night. Dead serious.

STAY ALIVE

BREAKDOWN

Who will survive?

The first thought Albert "Flash" Edwards, sixty-three, had when he felt the Milk Truck dying underneath him was, *I told you so.* He had told everyone he could think to tell that the Milk Truck, the van purchased from the St. Paul's School District at least a quarter of a century before, was too darn rickety to trust. Vans were well made, he knew, especially Fords, but all machines made by human hands had an earthly limit. That's what he thought. He had told the bosses of Camp Summertime, Dave and Margaret Waters, that the van needed to be junked and a new one bought. But did they listen? Of course they didn't. They told him the Milk Truck was a tradition and a part of camp lore.

No one listened to Flash Edwards. That was fact.

But, as usual, he was right about what he knew. He didn't pretend to know everything, but he knew engines, and he knew the Milk Truck better than any engine around, and he knew it was dying when they had turned onto Hundred Mile Road.

He heard one of the kids make a mocking sound – probably Tock, the troublemaker – when the van began to shake, and he glanced in the mirror quickly to tell him to knock it off. The Milk Truck had dignity, he wanted to say, and everything would get old one day, even them, but what good did it do to try and reason with spoiled kids? He shook his head and tried to lift the gearshift into a soft second, but the bus kicked and complained and began to grind.

His second thought was: *We're a lot of miles from somewhere, and a few miles from nowhere.*

The Hundred Mile Road wasn't called the Hundred Mile Road for nothing, he knew. That was another thing he would have told Margaret and Dave Waters if they had been standing in front of him. He would have said, you've got a girl here, Olivia, who has to get to California. You have another one, Maggie, who is going from here to LAX, then on to Japan for some sort of special exchange. Two of the boys, Preston and Simon, are heading out to the East Coast. You do not send a bus filled with kids hurrying to make a connection over the Hundred Mile Road and expect to wave good-bye and hop in your fancy Otter aircraft and head toward the Outer Banks as the Waterses did every autumn. You did not lock up the camp, lower the security gate behind the Milk Truck, and wave them off. No, you gave them first-class transportation and you supervised their travel and you made sure the itinerary made human sense. But not the Waterses. That wasn't how they saw the world. That wasn't the way things went at Camp Summertime.

"Hey!" someone yelled from the back of the bus. "Hey, what's going on?"

"Mind your knitting!" Flash said.

"What does that even mean?" Maggie asked.

"It means it's too hot to listen to you kids. Mind your own potatoes."

He didn't know for sure if he was talking to them or to himself or to the Milk Truck.

He gently put the gearshift back into first and tried to even her out with gas. But the Milk Truck started to shudder even harder. Then it wheezed and bucked and he knew the party was over. He eased the truck over to the side of the dirt road. Not that it mattered if he put her on the side of the road, he reflected. They were the last vehicle coming this way until the snowmobiles took it over in winter. Gates blocked the road from either end – that was steadfast rule the Waterses had instituted many years before – so that no drifters or joy riders could make it out to Camp Summertime and steal whatever they could carry. He had the key to both gates, and it was his job to take the last group out and lock the door behind him.

He gave the van one more squirt of gas, then listened to it pop three times in quick succession. He turned it off quickly and silence suddenly filled in the empty places. Then the van jerked a little to the right and the front tire crumpled on the shoulder of the road. A few trees dragged their bony fingers over the roof of the van and the forward momentum of the vehicle grinded them into a dull, teetering halt. They weren't going fast enough to cause any real damage, but the van sank a little on its axle as if it had settled down to die.

Then the kids began to clap.

"Do you people have any brains in your head?" Flash asked, his anger at the phony applause rising up him as quickly a bead of mercury in a thermometer. "Does even one person here have a particle of brain?"

It was too hot for this nonsense. Way too hot. He stood next to the steering wheel, his eyes moving over the passengers. He was tired of kids, he realized. It happened by the end of every summer.